"Awake my s[...]

Any other words of the hymn died in Nancy's throat when, about twenty feet away, the ward doors opened automatically and Woodrow Lawing walked through. With his head of dark, wavy hair, and wearing a navy blue suit and tie, the distinguished, handsome man was centered against a background of white walls, looking like he could be the answer to any woman's dream.

And of course that's all it had been.

A young girl's fantasy.

"...wake and sing..."

She wanted to. But her soul was no longer in control. Her emotions panicked. Her heart sang. But not about "the birth of Israel's King!"

For a moment her middle-aged being had no control over that young girl who still lived inside her. She watched Glenda approach Woody. They spoke briefly. Glenda gestured toward a room. He nodded, turned, and walked to the room more slowly than when he'd entered the third floor. After a few steps, he disappeared from her sight.

YVONNE LEHMAN

is an award-winning, bestselling author of 50 books, includ-ing mystery, romance, young adult, women's fiction, and mainstream historical. She founded and directed the Blue Ridge Mountains Christian Writers Conference for 25 years and now directs the Blue Ridge "Autumn in the Mountains" Novel Retreat, held annually at the Ridgecrest/LifeWay Conference Center near Asheville, NC.

Books by Yvonne Lehman

HEARTSONG PRESENTS

Let it Snow

Yvonne Lehman

Heartsong Presents

Thanks to Gail for the idea and Lori
for the pleurisy and personal information.

A note from the Author:

*I love to hear from my readers! You may correspond with
me by writing:*

Yvonne Lehman
Author Relations
P.O. Box 9048
Buffalo, NY 14240-9048

ISBN-13: 978-0-373-48644-1

LET IT SNOW

This edition issued by special arrangement with Barbour Publishing,
Inc., 1810 Barbour Drive, Uhrichsville, Ohio, U.S.A.

Chapter 1

*Christmas season—Silver City—small town
outside Washington, DC*

Nancy Walker Elrod's footsteps, breath, and peace of mind halted outside the doorway of her mother's kitchen.

Lyrics echoed in her mind:

Fifteen years ago and I still feel the same....

Surely her mother wasn't humming *that* song. Not that Nancy had anything against country music. Her mother introduced her to all kinds in their younger days. But this one she'd rather ignore. However, at this nostalgic time of year, conversations turned to the good ol' days and thoughts of past Christmas seasons.

The last two Christmases had been hard for her, without Ben. This year was easier, and Nancy had felt ready to come home again. At some point she needed to discuss the possibility of coming home...permanently. She could relate to her widowed mother in new and old ways.

The familiar aroma wafting into the hallway punctuated that point. Her mom's famous cookies were baking. Wheat flour replaced the former white. But the ingredients of apple sauce, walnuts, and chocolate chips were…*still the same.*

Nancy walked into the kitchen and laid her scarf and shoulder bag on a chair.

Her mother turned from the stove. "As soon as you find out anything more about Marge, let me know."

"I will." Nancy knew her mom was worried about her best friend. Staying busy and humming songs, usually hymns, were ways of coping.

Her mom sighed. "I should be there."

"Others are with her. And you know Mrs. Lawing was more concerned about that furry little mongrel than she was about herself." Nancy looked around. "Where is that dog anyway?"

Her mom gestured toward the back door but lifted her eyebrows. "Better not let Marge hear you call Sophie a mongrel…or a dog. She's sensitive about her little companion," she warned. "Sophie is more valuable to her than those cell phones are to the younger generation."

"Your cell phone was a convenience for you today."

"Well, yes. They're good for emergencies."

Today had been an emergency. Jean Walker and Marge Lawing had gone to a missionary program and luncheon at church. After eating, Mrs. Lawing complained of chest pains and shortness of breath. She blamed reflux, since she'd had that before. When her mom called Nancy, she insisted that Mrs. Lawing be taken to the doctor.

"I don't suppose they'd let her have any of these." Jean Walker set the freshly baked cookies on a cooling rack and lowered the pot holder to the countertop.

"No, Mom. Dr. Stevens' nurse said they're going to do additional testing at the hospital. That will take a while. But the EKG she had at the doctor's office showed no indication of heart trouble, and that's a good sign."

Her mom nodded and looked across at Nancy. "Well, I hope. Carl Stevens said he wants her tested for pneumonia, and he will call Woodrow." She paused. "He might be at the hospital, you know."

"He?"

"Woody."

Nancy turned from her mother's gaze and focused on her arm making its way into the jacket sleeve.

Woody.

Why did someone have to mention your name?

Another line of that song. Old memories threatened. Her mother hadn't hummed that line, but it made its way through the years and into Nancy's mind.

She glanced over when her mom said, "Hear that?" She reached over to the TV on a small shelf above the countertop and turned up the volume. "Getting down to freezing tonight. Better dress warm."

By that time Nancy had shrugged into her jacket. This was like the old days, too. Nancy didn't mind. She felt good being back in Silver City and feeling much like Mom's little girl again. She patted her pockets. "Gloves in here, and I have my scarf."

The weatherman finished his report. A commercial came on. Nancy glanced at the wall clock. "I'd better go."

"Cookies and hot coffee will be waiting. You know you can bring friends home."

Nancy knew she meant Woody. But he wasn't a friend. She'd ruined that years ago. But this house had always been a place where friends could congregate.

Fifteen, twenty, twenty-five years ago.

Through the years, however, her friends grew up and had families of their own.

Most…anyway.

"Thanks," she said. "I'll look in on Marge."

"Call and let me know how she is right away. And tell her I'm praying for her."

Nancy nodded. "I shouldn't be gone long." She wrapped the scarf around her neck and drew her keys from the shoulder bag then glanced at her mom picking up a cookie. "Save some for me, now."

"Only testing." Her mom grinned. "Have to make sure they're just right."

Nancy laughed. "They're always just right." She opened the back door, and Sophie, the saucy little shih tzu mix, scooted in and marched like she owned the place through the kitchen and into the hallway.

Jean Walker laughed. "Sophie likes the spot next to the fireplace. I'll go turn on the TV for her."

After saying "Bye," Nancy closed the kitchen door and stepped into the carport where her car was parked beside her mom's. She shivered but breathed deeply of the welcomed crisp fresh air.

On the fifteen-minute drive to the small hospital at the edge of Silver City, noticing that lights already decorated most businesses and many homes, she hummed the songs the choral group would sing. She didn't consider herself a great singer, but it was something her family had enjoyed.

She'd been pleased when asked to join the carolers who visited the hospital several evenings a week during the Christmas season.

She hadn't known that her mom's best friend would become ill.

She did know Woody would come if possible.

An audible gasp escaped her throat. She was no longer humming the carols but the one her mother had hummed.

Still feel the same? the lyric asked her.

Well, yes and no. A memory could pop into one's mind and spark feelings that produced laughter or tears. Like when she and her daughter, Rebekah, mentioned Ben. And of course, she couldn't dismiss Woody from her mind. After all, he'd been a vital part of her life—her family's lives—when she was young.

And in those days she'd never had what some spoke of as Plan A and Plan B.

She almost laughed aloud at that.

Her Plan A had been to act on impulse. Plan B was never much better.

But, she lectured herself, she was no longer impulsive, and it wasn't a Plan B that ruled her life, but God's plan.

God had blessed her with a man who had been just right for her. Now Ben was gone. But she had her mom. She had her brother, Jim, and his family. She had Rebekah, who would someday give her grandchildren.

Tonight she would try to bestow a little happiness and inspiration to patients in the hospital. Giving to others brought purpose and fulfillment in one's own life.

The Good Book had a reason for saying, "Love your neighbor as yourself."

She chuffed aloud. The only thing wrong with that was keeping it in context. Loving her neighbor had been where she went wrong in the first place.

The unbidden thought of *what if* often flitted through her mind.

But that changed nothing.

What was…*was!*

She pulled into a parking place in front of the small hospital and exercised Plan A, which was to exit the car with her shoulder bag and choir robe. The touch of her remote and the ensuing beep ensured the doors locked. With a determined stride, she entered through the automatic doors and met the carolers in the lobby.

Plan B was to simply think and behave like a mature woman, regardless. There was no reason in the world for her throat and heart to act up at the thought of the man who didn't want her...never had.

She did have the foresight to accompany that thought with a little prayer.

Chapter 2

While riding the elevator to the third floor with Pastor Jameson and five carolers, Nancy's apprehension changed to anticipation of seeing Glenda. They'd become friends and confidantes when they'd worked there during nurses' training years ago. They'd kept in touch and whenever they met, although it might not be for years, they shared any big changes that had taken place in their lives.

As soon as the doors to the third floor opened, they rushed to embrace. They'd spoken briefly on the phone earlier, but duty had called for Glenda, now a charge nurse. When the warm hug ended, Glenda looked at the carolers and back at Nancy. "Come into the lounge. You can change into your robe and leave your things in there."

Nancy did, and all the while each was telling the other how she still looked the same. "We always do," Nancy teased. She was still a brunette and Glenda a blue-eyed blond, and they didn't have to say how they kept their hair that way. "Others our age change, but not us."

Glenda laughed. Yes, like old times. They would get serious later.

For now, Nancy's thoughts turned to Marge. "Do you know any more about Mrs. Lawing?"

"She's just come back from having additional tests. We don't have the results yet. We have her ready for any IVs, and she's on oxygen."

Nancy sighed. "My mom really wants to be here."

Glenda shook her head. "You know how tiring a hospital visit can be for a patient," she said, to which Nancy nodded. "Mrs. Lawing begged a couple of friends and Mrs. Jameson to leave. You might let her rest awhile before going in to talk to her."

Nancy agreed that sounded best, and she changed into the white robe with the red satin V-stole that draped over her shoulders. They returned to the hall, and she joined the singers assembled at one side of the area so they wouldn't be in the way of any activity. Glenda allowed employees who weren't hindered by their duties to gather at the nurses' station. Pastor Jameson stood at the partition, smiling, nodding as the group sang, "Silent Night."

After that one, they began, "Awake my soul, awake—"

Any other words of the hymn died in Nancy's throat when, about twenty feet away, the ward doors opened automatically and Woodrow Lawing walked through. With his head of dark, wavy hair, and wearing a navy blue suit and tie, the distinguished, handsome man was centered against a background of white walls, looking like he could be the answer to any woman's dream.

And of course that's all it had been.

A young girl's fantasy.

"…wake and sing…"

She wanted to. But her soul was no longer in control. Her emotions panicked. Her heart sang. But not about "the birth of Israel's King!"

For a moment her middle-aged being had no control over that young girl who still lived inside her. She watched Glenda approach Woody. They spoke briefly. Glenda gestured toward a room. He nodded, turned, and walked to the room more slowly than when he'd entered the third floor. After a few steps, he disappeared from her sight.

Nancy stood mute, like a lost chord. She leaned toward the hymnal Susan held, pretending she couldn't see the words or had lost her place. Then she realized it wasn't just her place she'd lost. She'd lost her mind.

"You okay?" Susan whispered.

Nancy grimaced and pointed to her throat. Susan smiled sympathetically and continued singing.

When the others finished, those at the nurses' station applauded. Glenda approached the choral group and held out a sheet of paper to Delores, the choir leader. "I wrote down the names and room numbers of patients who'd love to have you come in and sing." Her smiled faded. "One said she could hear without your coming in but said to thank you. Another would not be able to respond. And"—she glanced over her shoulder and back again—"room 342 has a visitor right now. She's struggling, so it's best if you sing outside her room."

Delores thanked her and took the sheet of paper. "All right, gang. That was great. Let's go across to 335." She waved them across the hall while Nancy stood still.

"You're not coming?" Delores asked.

"Remember I told you I needed to visit someone. That's why I drove my car instead of riding in the van."

"I remember," Delores said in her pleasant way. "We're just glad to have you sing with us whenever you will."

"She has a throat problem, too," Susan said.

Delores nodded. "Well, if the cold weather doesn't do it to you, this is the place to catch something." She laughed at the irony of it. "See you later. You take care of yourself now."

For a moment, Nancy felt guilty about the throat problem.

Then it occurred to her that's exactly what she had. She often had the problem of the wrong words at the wrong time, or a lack of right words at the right time.

As soon as the others went into the room and began singing, Glenda slid her arm around Nancy's waist. "Want something for that throat?"

The sidelong look Glenda gave her said she suspected the throat problem was a farce. Nancy walked faster. "I'm okay." She wanted to change the subject and the thought process. "Let's see what Pastor Jameson has there."

"Those are boxes he had delivered earlier," Glenda said.

They walked up to the partition where the pastor was taking an object from the box.

"Oh, how precious." Nancy held out her hand. He placed the small snow globe in her palm. "These for the patients?"

"Patients and nurses," he said. "There are plenty. After the group sings, I'll go into the rooms and take a globe and maybe strike up a conversation."

"Wonderful idea." Nancy knew he meant it would be an opportunity to talk about the real meaning of Christmas. Might be a good idea to have something in her hand when… if…she talked to Woody.

Oh, but of course she'd talk to him. Not to would be the height of impropriety.

She cleared her throat. "They're not going to sing in 342. I know Mrs. Lawing. Could I take the globe to her?"

"I would appreciate a little help." His face darkened. "You're not singing anymore?"

Glenda spoke up. "She has a throat problem."

He gave a warning look. "Don't want the patients to catch anything now, do we?"

"She's not contagious."

Nancy brought her hand up to her mouth, hoping not to laugh about Glenda speaking up for her, but she was glad. She didn't care to stretch the truth to the pastor. He'd probably put her on the prayer list and have the entire church pray for her.

That might not be a bad idea.

The pastor lifted a globe from the box. Smiling, he headed down the hall.

Nancy stared at the globe in her hand.

Glenda's voice was gentle. "Are you going to take that in?"

"Sure." She tried to shrug but didn't dare meet Glenda's eyes. "Right now."

She only had to put one foot in front of the other. She managed to get to the door, deciding to say, quietly of course, *"Hello. How are you? Haven't seen you in a while."*

No, that didn't feel right.

"Hi. I don't mean to disturb you, but I thought I'd bring in—"

Yuck.

Maybe she should just say hi and leave the rest up to him. But what if he only said hi back, or nothing, or didn't recognize her, or…

By then she'd reached the door, which wasn't completely closed, and pushed it farther open. He sat in a chair, his back to her. She could see the outline of a light blue shirt at the back of his neck. She didn't know about the tie. When he'd walked through the door its color hadn't registered, but she knew everything would match. It was his face that drew her. The handsome, concerned face. He'd looked like he could use a friend. But that stopped being a possibility a long, long time ago.

His shoulders were still broad. Oh, how stupid. What else would they be? His hair might be a tad thinner, maybe not. She might…touch his shoulder?

Oh, how heartless could she be? Here was a man in distress about his ailing mother, and she hadn't thought about what she might say to comfort him.

Chapter 3

"I want to give you this…"

Woodrow Lawing sat in the chair he'd pulled up to the hospital bed. He didn't turn to see who came into the room and whispered those words. Why whisper? If a voice could restore his mother to good health, then he would welcome shouting.

He hardly glanced at the feminine hand that placed what she'd called *this* on the bedside table. Was likely the nurse he'd spoken with. He knew, at times like this, people tried to show they cared. But he needed more than people to care. He needed a miracle. It was Christmas, and his mom was all he had. He could hardly bear to see her sick.

Hearing the soft footsteps fade, Woodrow gazed at the object on the table.

A snow globe?

Someone wanted him to have, of all things, a snow globe?

He stared. The small Nativity scene inside the glass circle represented a night of miracles.

A light scoff escaped his throat. He wasn't a skeptic. He believed in God, and the baby in that manger. But he'd seen too many things go wrong in his life to believe God would step in now like some fairy godfather, sprinkle him with magic white powder, and let him live happily ever after.

He focused on his mother again. She didn't look like the same strong woman he'd seen a little more than a week ago. Although in her mid-seventies, she'd maintained good health. She believed diet and exercise kept her well. When he'd related his plans to take her to *The Nutcracker* Christmas ballet, opening in DC on Thanksgiving weekend, she'd asked if they could postpone it and have a simple dinner somewhere in Silver City. She'd said her reflux was acting up.

They'd had a quiet dinner at the Knight Hotel. He supposed he took her more for granted than he should, expecting her to always be with him because he didn't want to think otherwise. When he'd called a few days ago, she had a cold. Everyone had colds now and then so neither was concerned.

But today, Carl Stevens, their family doctor for many years, called to say she'd been admitted to the hospital for tests. He suspected pneumonia. He assured Woodrow that his mom was not in grave danger, she'd just contracted something they would identify and deal with.

But somehow neither the diagnosis nor prognosis exactly reassured Woodrow. Carl said he'd meet him at the hospital and talk with him.

Woodrow arranged for another professor to handle his classes' final exams the following day and didn't take time to drive to his Georgetown condo, but drove straight to the hospital.

About half an hour later, the nurse in the hallway said his mom had been given medication to help her rest better. But when he entered the room, he knew that was not a woman at rest.

Her eyes didn't open. Her chest rose and fell with each wheeze that struggled for breath through her open mouth.

The bluish tint of her lips was only a shade lighter than the circles beneath her eyes. Her pale face appeared clammy.

Many years ago she'd complained when gray hairs began to streak her black hair. Now, uncharacteristically disheveled and damp, a few black hairs streaked the gray. The color had reversed.

He'd heard the role of parent and child reverses, too. If she'd stay with him, he'd gladly take on that privilege. No matter where he'd lived, or visited, or how long he'd been away, he always took comfort in coming home to Mom. As he saw her in that fragile state, he realized what it would mean to really lose her someday.

Seeing that her fist clutched the sheet, he reached over and gently loosened her grip. Her fingers felt cold, but her palm was sweaty. He moved her arm down by her side and placed her hand between both of his.

He loved her more in her weakness than in her strength. Was that the way of God? If so, Woodrow knew he was loved considerably. He'd rarely felt weaker.

"I'm here, Mom. You're going to be all right. We can get through this together."

Trying to concentrate on anything else, he looked over at the bedside table and picked up the little snow globe. It contained a symbol of hope. *But, Mom. The doctor doesn't even know what's going on with you. That's not fair.*

He knew fairness had nothing to do with it. Life wasn't made up of fairness, but facts.

Reason told him she'd had a good life. She always said that, even after her husband died. She'd said, "Woody, I had a good marriage with your dad. I miss him, but I can't complain. God blessed us in so many ways. The most important way was you."

Woodrow reminded himself that Carl said this didn't appear to be serious. But it *looked* serious. His mother was lying in a hospital bed, gasping for breath, and with IVs ready to be hooked up if needed. It brought back memories.

He felt the loss of his dad anew. He'd seen his dad's emphysema progress to the point of having to live with taking an oxygen tank around with him. Later, even that wasn't enough. Woodrow couldn't release his grief. Tears stung his eyes but wouldn't fall. Emotion choked his throat, but he couldn't dislodge it. Pain hurt his pounding heart, but he couldn't quiet it. Grumbles complained in his stomach, but he'd lost his appetite.

He looked at the globe again. The baby Jesus no longer slept on the hay in that manger. He lived in heaven, waiting for Woodrow's mother.

"I need her more than You do," Woodrow said aloud. "I just can't go home to that empty house. I have no one." The weight of the years lay heavy on him, as if his life were flashing before him.

To keep his mind from dwelling on the negative, he searched for diversion and picked up the globe. He shook it in a *no-no-no* gesture as he thought the words.

He watched the snow fall around that little manger scene of husband, wife, and child. A family like he'd wanted but never had.

He remembered another snow…twenty-five years ago…

Chapter 4

Twenty-five years earlier...the Christmas season

*W*hack!

The impact took Woody's breath away.

He wiped away the cold, icy snowball that had hit him squarely on the side of his face. He took off his glove and gently felt his cold nose with his warm thumb and forefinger. It didn't seem to be broken. He wiped across his nostrils with his finger to check if he had a nosebleed. Apparently not—just more ice.

Seventeen-year-old Nancy Walker jumped out from behind the snowman in her front yard, looking much like a snowman herself in that white down jacket with the fur-trimmed hood around her face. Her laughter formed a filmy mist in the frigid air.

"I thought you went inside," he growled playfully. With a threatening look, he slipped his hand back into his glove, reached down, and scooped up snow to form into a ball.

Nancy shrieked, tromped through the snow, and hid behind the big maple tree.

Stealthily, Woody approached the tree, ready to fling the snowball on either side when she emerged.

She didn't try to escape, however, but peeked out from behind the tree and taunted, "Whatever happened to your Boy Scout motto, 'Be Prepared'?"

Woody quickly stepped around the tree. "Gotcha!" He pinned her to the tree with his left hand holding on to her shoulder and his right arm drawn back in pitching position.

Nancy didn't laugh, nor look playful, but gazed at him with an expression he'd never seen on her face. For an instant he wondered about that motto himself. He wasn't prepared. Caught off guard, he had to remind himself this was Nancy, the little sister of his best friend, Jim.

She was a friend, like all the other kids in this residential neighborhood. He needed to at least smear her face with the icy mix, but she stopped his intention with another question.

"Now that you've caught me, what are you going to do with me?"

Woody's breath caught in his throat, then it drifted from him like a ghostly warm mist quivering in the snowy night. Everything in the whitewashed world faded except her brown eyes, soft with challenge, gazing up at him.

Somewhere in the back of his mind, he knew he had a girlfriend in college that he'd been anxious to get back to after this family visit during the holidays. He always enjoyed seeing his lifelong friends. But his ambitions were being drawn elsewhere, toward career and new acquaintances and possibilities.

But Nancy had asked what he was going to do with her.

The Woody of a moment ago would have shown her. He would have given her a taste of that snowball along with an icy face wash. Or even managed to get it to her neck and cause it to trickle down her chest. She'd wiggle and scream and try to shake the snow down or pat it to make it melt, and he would laugh and laugh. Then they'd have a snowball fight, darting from tree to tree until they became exhausted enough to go inside or some neighbor came out on a porch and they'd duck behind a tree, holding in their laughter until the neighbor went inside. Then they'd say, "Bye," and go to their own homes.

He'd smile all the way home and think about childhood and friends and neighbors and families and the meaning of Christmas and peace on earth for a while and wonder why he ever wanted to get back to a hectic life of preparing for the future. This was the good life. Church reminded him of a few things he needed to reconsider in his life. But he'd go back to the rat race and again be a part of the crowd who had to have its fun in between studying and the pressure of the rest of their lives.

But in a moment, Nancy's question changed everything. How would he answer her?

He was used to college girls and their innuendos. He knew all about flirting and meaningful glances and between-the-lines speech.

But from Nancy?

The hood with white fur around the edges surrounded her face, covering all but a bit of dark hair peeking out at her forehead. Her dainty nose was red from the cold and her cheeks pink against her smooth, fair skin. Through the bare branches of the maple tree, white powdery snow filtered down upon her long black lashes that formed a canopy over her dark brown, questioning eyes.

Her generous pink lips were parted. The mist of her breath mingled with his. Little puffs of breath indicated a fast heartbeat. Like his own? From the activity of having run? He didn't think so.

What to do with Nancy?

Something inside him, or in her eyes, seemed to say she wasn't a little girl anymore. He'd known that in his mind for years. They'd talked about how each had changed and grown during the months they didn't see each other. There had been no overt attempt to see each other. Living on the same block, with one house between them, and her brother, Jim, being his best friend, made constant contact unavoidable.

He dropped the snowball when her gloved hand reached up and drew his face down to hers. Maybe the snow froze his brain. But not his emotions. Like a block of ice, melting, he moved slowly toward her, bent his face closer to her. Her eyes spoke of happiness, and her lips invited his.

He'd never before tasted such icy, cold, sweet, warm lips in his life. The warmth spread through his being, into his veins, into his heart, eliminating all reason, until she threw her arms around his neck and declared, "Oh, Woody. I love you. I've always loved you."

He felt as if that snowball had whacked him again. He wished it had. He wished his nose had been broken.

He moved her arms away. She stepped back against the tree again. Her face crumbled, and she lowered her gaze to the ground. Her sweet lips trembled.

Should he have seen this coming?

He told himself no. During holidays, college students from church and some from school had parties, went to movies, out to eat, or gathered at someone's parents' home. Nancy joined in when they met at Jim's house.

She was one of the crowd only at her own house. She was… Nancy. A good friend.

But…good friends don't kiss—unless it's a peck on the lips or the cheek.

Why had he kissed her?

Could he blame it on her? She had put her arms around his neck and pulled him close. But he was older, and experienced in such matters.

She said she loved him.

Love?

He knew about high school crushes. At seventeen, he'd thought himself grown-up enough to know life's answers. After going to college, however, he realized he didn't even know all the questions. And now boys and girls in high school looked like kids to him.

And yet, he knew this kind of thing happened all the time. Kids fell in love with their brother's best friend. It happened in novels and in movies. A young girl growing up and falling in love with love. Puppy love. Crush.

But, he knew it was serious, too. He'd been head over heels about the little Shirley Temple–looking girl named Janie Fulsom in the first grade. Seeing her had made his heart thump like a big bass drum. Even now in college, a special girl could make his head spin and his heart speed.

Nancy was only seventeen, a senior in high school. He was twenty-three and a senior in college.

He had to say something before she ran away and their friendship would be destroyed forever.

"Nancy," he said as gently as he could, holding on to the sleeve of her white jacket. "No one could receive a better compliment than that. Since you were born, you and I have loved each other. We've been friends in spite of our age difference. I think the world of you."

She stiffened as if frozen. He hated this, but he didn't know what else to say. He refused to take his hand from her arm, lest she run away. He couldn't let her flee in embarrassment. He was flattered. But she was a teenager. He was a man.

"Right now, Nancy, we both have to concentrate on finishing our education. You're not even out of high school. This is not something we can even consider right now."

He felt her trembling beneath the thick down jacket. No, he told himself, these were not trembles but shivers from the frigid air.

"You understand, Nancy?"

She nodded, and her shaky lips almost formed a smile.

What could he say? How could he redeem the situation? They'd always hugged when he'd come home after being gone for a while. Both their families were huggers. "Give me a hug?"

This time she didn't reach around his neck but around his chest. He held her loosely, although feeling her press against him. Had she always held him that tightly? He'd never thought about what kind of hug she gave him any more than he thought about the kind her mom gave him. It was…a hug from a friend. He patted the back of Nancy's jacket, like one would pat a dog, then stepped away.

Her arms fell away from him. She gazed up into his face. He saw the spark of light in her eyes. No, she wasn't offended. She still…liked him.

But she was only a high school girl, growing up. He just happened along at a weak moment.

"You better get inside before you freeze to death," he said.

"Good night," she said softly and smiled in a way he had never before noticed.

That was different, too. They always said, "Bye," if they said anything at all. But she stepped away from the tree, and her boots made soft squishy sounds in the snow.

Woody knew what he had to do.

He reached down and grabbed a glove full of snow and formed it into a ball. It smacked her in the back. She screamed and scooped up snow in her white gloves. Inching sideways toward her porch, she threw it at him.

He ducked. The next one she pitched from her porch hit him in the chest. He laughed and brushed it off as he walked on toward his house. He waited for a moment after hearing her screen door squeak.

His ploy hadn't really worked. He'd hoped to recapture the fun they'd had yesterday when he, Jim, Nancy, and a couple of neighborhood kids had built the snowman. Tonight, he felt he and Nancy had just gone through the motions of former times.

"Go on," he said. "You know I have to see you safely inside." He reached down as if to gather more snow.

"Yiii," she screeched then opened the front door. Light framed her in the doorway, making a halo of the fur around her face. Then she closed the door, leaving the porch in shadow from the overhanging roof.

Woody's shoes crunched against the snow, now a couple of inches thick as he walked slowly home, watching the ground. He stopped for a moment and looked at the streetlight and the snowflakes filtering down through its golden glow. He heard the silence. Snow was quiet.

The world was hushed.

No sound at all, except his heartbeat in his ears.

White rooftops blended with the landscape. Roads and driveways had become a sea of white. Christmas lights shone from windows, and smoke curled from chimneys. But outside there was no sign of life, except his warm breath misting in the snowy air.

He'd come home to be with family and friends.

The cold, hard truth struck like that snowball in his face. He thought of the irony. Tonight, he'd lost a friend—because of love.

Chapter 5

Nancy walked from Mrs. Lawing's room and back to the nurses' station where Glenda was watching the snow in one of the little globes. She returned it to the box and lifted her eyebrows at Nancy in a questioning way. "That was quick," she said.

Nancy shook her head, clasping her hands in front of her, lest they reveal the shakiness she felt inside. "It didn't seem the time to strike up a conversation."

Glenda opened her mouth to speak, but the rush of the opening doors claimed their attention. Emergencies could be expected at any time.

But entering the floor was another man dressed in a suit and tie. Nancy recognized Dr. Carl Stevens, although she'd known him best when he'd worn a white lab coat. He was a doctor when she became a nurse at the hospital many years ago. He was in private practice now, and her mother's physician.

"Nancy," he said, walking up. "Good to see you again.

And thanks for having your mom bring Mrs. Lawing to my office. Both those women tend to ignore any symptoms of illness, as if that will make them go away."

They smiled about that.

He addressed Glenda. "Any change with Mrs. Lawing?"

"No, but she's had her fever reducer and pain medication." She turned to the nurse behind the station.

"I'll get her chart," the nurse said.

His kind eyes focused on Nancy again. "Are you singing solo for the patients?" He lifted his hand again. "Ah, but now I hear other voices." The sweet tones of "O Little Town of Bethlehem" wafted out through an open door.

"I sang with the others a little while ago," she said, feeling uneasy, as if she were lying. "But I also came to see Mrs. Lawing."

"Her son is with her now," Glenda said as the nurse handed Dr. Stevens the chart.

His eyes skimmed the chart for a moment, then he turned to Glenda. "I have the strictest confidence that you all know what you're doing. But I've known Mrs. Lawing and her son for a long time. I came to talk with him."

He handed her the chart then turned toward the room.

Glenda sighed. "Not every doctor would make a special trip like this."

Nancy agreed. "He's a good man." She paused. "Why did he ask about my singing?"

Glenda tugged on her open sleeve. "Maybe because you're wearing a choir robe?"

Nancy chuffed. "I forgot I was wearing it."

"If you're not going to sing anymore, take off the robe." Glenda looked at another nurse. "Phyllis, I'll be in the lounge attending to important business."

"Oh, coffee time," Phyllis said and laughed.

"Exactly."

In the lounge, Nancy lifted the stole over her head and

folded it. She unhooked the fastener at the back of the robe, slipped out of the soft material, folded it, and laid it on the coffee table.

By that time, the coffeepot was gurgling and dripping. The rich aroma whetted Nancy's taste buds. The couch and easy chair beckoned, too. But she couldn't relax yet. She had a mission. She needed to visit with Marge Lawing, even if the woman wouldn't know it. She needed to speak to Woody.

Glenda took a couple of cups from a cabinet. Nancy remembered that her friend never liked coffee in a foam cup. Neither did she, for that matter. She pulled up the sleeves of the white cashmere sweater that she wore with her jeans. Glenda was watching the pot so Nancy sank into the padded chair, her sweater reminding her of a white jacket…a lifetime ago…when she believed Woody loved her.

Twenty-five years earlier… the Christmas season

He loves me.

Nancy stood on her porch, holding on to the screen door for a moment, watching Woody stand motionless, looking at her, until he told her to go inside. She didn't really plan to tell him she loved him, but the moment seemed so right.

Yesterday's snow had become hard packed, and salt made slush on the roads. Then a fresh snow had fallen before they left for church. After the Christmas program, adults were eager to drive home before the roads became slick again. The young people wanted to walk. Nancy's mom and dad said that was fine after Jim and Woody offered to walk with the younger ones.

After the last of her friends had gone into their homes, she and Woody walked two blocks before reaching her house. She might not see him again until spring break.

She had always loved him. She analyzed the emotion—thought about everything she knew about love, any feelings she'd ever had about a boy—and none of it measured up to the feelings she had for Woody.

They were right for each other.

She knew it.

She also knew he was right about the age thing.

Her parents would ground her until she reached twenty-one before they'd let her date an older man, even if their families had been friends forever.

Woody hadn't exactly said he loved her. But then, being the Christian man he was, and a gentleman, he would never take advantage of her love. He said he'd always loved her. He had to tack on that *friend* part, since they had to wait.

She went into the house.

Her mom walked in from the kitchen, holding a dishcloth. "I expected you home before now. I was starting to get worried. Where's Jim?"

"He walked Lauren home."

Her dad lowered his magazine and peered at her over his reading glasses.

She looked from her dad to her mom. "Woody walked with me and the other guys."

"Oh, okay." Her mom smiled. Her dad nodded and lifted his magazine to reading height.

No, neither of them would suspect she and Woody were in love.

"I'm freezing," Nancy said. "I need to get into my flannel pajamas."

"Okay, dear," her mom said. "There's hot chocolate and cider, you know. When Jim gets here, we'll open our presents."

"Thanks, Mom." Her mom and dad had always let her and Jim open one present on Christmas Eve when they were small, and they still followed that tradition. Tonight, she felt she'd already gotten the most wonderful present one could get. She'd been in the arms of the man she loved, and they kissed.

She went into her bedroom at the front of the frame house, closed the door, then hurried to the side window. Maybe she could get one more glimpse of the love of her life. Yes, he stood silhouetted against the glow of the streetlight while the soft snow fell all around him.

Was he seeing what she saw? Nancy viewed the scene as a pristine representation of what lay ahead for her and Woody. Her world was adorned in its white wedding dress. Christmas lights, behind filmy windows, provided the colorful bridal bouquet. Snowflakes, falling softly from the sky, reminded her of a bride looking at her beloved through a veil of lace.

Nancy removed her gloves and traced her lips with her fingers, remembering.

Yes, Woody. Knowing that you love me makes all the difference.

I can wait.

True love...can wait.

Chapter 6

Nancy rose from the chair and out of her contemplative mode when Glenda said, "Here you go," and was pouring a cup of the freshly brewed coffee.

Nancy walked over to the table and stirred in nondairy creamer. She really hadn't paid much attention to the lounge's furnishings when she'd worked here as a young nurse. She assumed there had been changes, but now she saw it as a comfortable reprieve from dealing with sick patients and tired feet.

"Thanks." She took a sip. "Good." She smiled at her friend who then poured her own cup.

"I'd love to sit here and talk, but with all that's going on, I probably should be visible, as if I'm in charge."

Nancy laughed. "That is your title."

Glenda raised her eyebrows, and they went out to the nurses' station. "Come on back." She pulled up a chair near hers and they sat.

Seeing the monitors, hearing the sounds, Nancy felt that moment of uncertainty again. The private nursing job she'd taken after Ben died had recently ended. She was neither a nurse nor a pastor's wife anymore. She supposed that meant she was at loose ends. But this wasn't the time to try to figure any of that out. She took another sip of coffee then glanced at Glenda. "Mrs. Lawing is having a rough time, isn't she?"

Glenda glanced away from a monitor and nodded. "All those tests are enough to wear anybody down. And not knowing the source of the problem adds stress. That aggravates any problem." She shook her head. "And, she is in her seventies."

"You never know," Nancy said. "Ben was only forty-one. His heart just gave out." She smiled at Glenda, who had sent a sweet letter of condolence after hearing about Ben.

"That's why it's so important to appreciate our family—" Glenda's voice caught. "While they're living."

Nancy nodded, recalling that Glenda and her husband divorced many years ago. And Glenda lost her mom about a year before Ben died. "You're right," Nancy said. "Rebekah and I became closer after Ben was gone from our lives." She gave a light laugh of irony. "We try to teach our children to be mature and responsible. Then when they are, we are left alone and lonely."

"What do you mean?" Glenda asked.

"Oh, only that Rebekah is staying in a dorm this year, instead of with me. And"—Nancy took a deep breath—"she and her boyfriend are talking about going to the mission field as soon as she's out of college."

"Oh, how wonderful." Glenda's eyes met Nancy's, and she grimaced. "But not for you."

Nancy shook her head briefly. "Since Ben's death the church has been so good." She sighed. "But I'm no longer the preacher's wife. I have to rethink my role in life." She sipped her coffee. "How is your sister?"

Just as Glenda opened her mouth to respond, a beep sounded. "Oops, that beep's for me." She stood and walked out into the hallway and into a room. Hearing commotion,

Nancy looked out and saw Pastor Jameson exit a room. Just then Dr. Stevens and Woody came from Mrs. Lawing's room, talking in low tones and heading straight for her. Nancy stood and walked down to the box of snow globes, thinking she needed to be doing something instead of standing there.

However, Pastor Jameson engaged Woody and Dr. Stevens in conversation. Woody seemed lost in thought for a moment, his shoulders lifted slightly, then he looked around. Nancy looked at the box of snow globes. She reached out and touched the top of one but wouldn't dare pick it up.

She heard Woody say, "Excuse me. I'll be with you in a moment."

He was heading her way.

When he reached the partition, he said, "Nancy."

Her eyes met his. He looked glad to see her, but not over-joyed. Just, like seeing someone he'd known a long time ago. She wasn't sure if he was uncomfortable or if that was just her own feelings. "Carl said you were here."

"Yes," she said.

"Are you working here?" His brief glance took in her white sweater and then swept back to her face. "But you're not in uniform."

"No, I'm not working here. I came to spend the holidays with Mom."

He nodded. "Jim told me a few weeks ago that your family would be in Silver City this Christmas." What did that quick flash in his eyes mean? Did he think she knew he'd be here and she was still chasing him? No. He wouldn't think that. Not after all these years. She didn't want him to think that. "I'm singing with the choral group."

Oh dear. But she was standing behind the nurses' station partition. "I mean, I was."

What do you say to an old friend? But he's not a friend to whom you say, "Come join us for a cup of coffee." And he's not old. He's...*Woody*.

His head dipped slightly, and his hand came near his mouth as he cleared his throat. His eyes held an amused look. Probably thinking, *Same ol' Nancy.*

He reverted to his reserved expression, no smile, as if he had to conceal that little silver spark in his deep blue eyes visible beneath those long dark lashes. Then she saw something else. The tired circles under his eyes. The little lines of strain in the whites of his eyes.

He looked tired, concerned, and of course, he would be.

"I'm so sorry about your mother," she said.

"Thank you. For that and for having your mom take her to the doctor." That worried look blanketed his face. Glenda returned, and Nancy appreciated her nearness.

Woody spoke again, to Glenda. "Dr. Stevens and I are going to the cafeteria."

Glenda nodded. "I'll notify you if there's any change."

"I'll sit with her until you get back," Nancy said. She thought she'd better add, "I came tonight to see her." She didn't want him to think she was there because she knew he would come to see his mom. Didn't want him to think she was stalking him. "My mom wants me to tell her she's praying for her."

His face softened. "Thank you. She would like that. And I appreciate it."

Glenda added, "We have the monitors right here. And I'll go in often."

He looked relieved, turned, and strode down the hall to Dr. Stevens.

While Nancy stared at the closed doors, Glenda spoke. "Looks like everything's under control. Shall we finish our coffee?"

Nancy walked over to the chair, took a swallow of the tepid coffee, and set it aside. She looked across at Glenda. "That was awkward. I haven't learned a thing in all these years."

"You said all the right things."

Said the right things? Nancy had no idea what she'd said.

She shrugged. "This is silly. But…even though it was years ago, after being rejected, it's still awkward."

"Did he never marry?"

"Not unless it's been recent. But I'm sure Mom or Jim would have let me know."

"Maybe not, with your grieving about Ben."

Nancy nodded. "True. They might think that it's not the time. But Ben died over two years ago. And besides, my family didn't know how I felt about Woody."

Glenda's jaw dropped. "You gotta be kidding. I mean, you weren't exactly silent about it."

"Well…" Nancy felt warmth rise in her face. "Maybe they did. But they figured I outgrew it."

"You did marry and have a child."

"Yes, I loved Ben. It was a good marriage. I needed to be loved, and he loved me so completely."

Glenda smiled. "Have you and Woody avoided each other through the years?"

"Just went our separate ways like people do. I've lived in North Carolina for ten years. Of course, we've both been in Silver City at the same time, but I'd be with my family, he with his, and we'd speak. All our serious conversations ended after he rejected me, though." She shrugged. "But that was such a long time ago."

Nancy tried to laugh, but Glenda spoke seriously. "Rejection hurts."

"Glenda?" Nancy saw her friend blink away tears. "What is it? Surely you're not upset over my childish antics twenty years ago."

"No, no. It's Helen. My sister. The snow globes reminded me of her."

Nancy remembered that Glenda had been a child of her parents' middle age. Her sister was much older.

"We haven't spoken in…" Glenda's attention focused on a monitor. "We'll talk later. I'm needed."

"I need to sit with Mrs. Lawing, too." Nancy walked down the hall and into room 342. She was a nurse, accustomed to the smells of medicine, disinfectant, sweating bodies, and the sounds of a struggle to breathe. She was aware of losses, different kinds, degrees. It seemed her best days were behind her.

Sitting in the chair where Woody had sat, looking at the woman who had given him life, she thought of Marge Lawing having seen better days, too. Maybe she could stop thinking of the past long enough to be of some help to the people she'd long ago thought would be her future.

But hadn't been.

And now, her future seemed so uncertain.

Chapter 7

Woody learned long ago not to expect a gourmet dinner when going through a college cafeteria line and felt much the same about hospital food. He made his choices of what looked most appetizing, and this evening, nothing really did. He'd been spoiled by the eclectic array of food in the DC area and abroad. When he wanted fresh lobster, shrimp, or crab they were readily available. And, he'd learned to cook and rather enjoyed that, particularly when sharing it with friends and colleagues.

This evening his mind focused on seeing his mother looking so frail and Nancy looking so…well. She always was pretty and had matured into a lovely woman. But he'd pushed her into the back of his mind and his heart a long time ago. Or rather, she'd forced him to do that.

But now was the time to follow Carl to a table with his tray and listen to the doctor's diagnosis.

"It doesn't seem to be a heart problem," Carl said, and the immediate thought came to Woody, *Is he talking about my heart, or my mom's? Let's hope he's right about either, or both.*

As they ate, Carl explained his reasons for his opinion. "In my office, the EKG didn't reveal any heart abnormality. But her breathing, and sharp pains when doing so, indicates there's something wrong in the right lung."

That brought cancer to Woody's mind. It seemed about as prevalent as the common cold.

Carl added, "The referral for a chest X-ray is to see if it's possibly pneumonia. The report should come from the lab soon. We'll see what that reveals."

Woody shook his head at the thought of pneumonia. This didn't sound good at all.

Carl didn't seem overly concerned. "However," he said, "the doctors here, and I, are leaning toward pleurisy."

"Pleurisy?" Woody wasn't familiar with that term. "What is that? How serious?"

Carl laid down his burger, swallowed, and took a gulp of coffee. "It's not as serious as having a heart attack, and pleurisy is treatable. However, it can be very painful. It occurs in degrees. Right now she's on an anti-inflammatory drug and pain meds."

At the moment, there was nothing to do but wait. The conversation turned more personal as they caught up on what each had been doing since they last saw each other, what was happening at Georgetown with Woody's students, and what was happening with Carl in Silver City.

Only a few miles separated the two, but it was like two different worlds: the big city and the small town. If things didn't go well with his mother, his connection with Silver City would be lost. Those nostalgic times of coming home, remembering what might have been, then being rejected and knowing what would never be. Memories were…bittersweet.

When they were into their second cups of coffee, Carl got a call. He thanked the caller then looked across at Woody.

"The chest X-ray results are in. She doesn't have pneumonia. We'll see how things go tonight, and I'll come first thing in the morning and check on her."

Carl seemed pleased, so Woody tried to be. He laid his paper napkin on the tray. "I should get back to Mom. And I don't want to keep Nancy waiting."

Well why not? crossed his mind. *I'd done that for years... until she tired of waiting.*

He and Carl took their trays to the rolling track at the kitchen window then rode the elevator to the third floor. A doctor came from his mother's room, and Carl introduced him as Dr. Sloan, who spoke with them for a moment. "I've given Mrs. Lawing the report," he said.

"She's awake?" Woody asked.

Dr. Sloan grinned. "Propped up and talking."

Woody hurried in, followed by Carl and Dr. Sloan. Nancy sat in the chair. The charge nurse smiled and stepped back.

His mom wasn't exactly propped up but was slanted with another pillow behind her head, looking disheveled and gray-faced, but she flashed him a tolerant glance. "The doctor thinks I'll live." She made a laugh sound but stopped it and said, "Oops. Mustn't do that."

Nancy started to rise. Woody motioned for her to stay seated. "You must be good medicine."

"Not me," she said. "The medication was good medicine."

They all laughed lightly, except his mom, who smiled faintly. "I don't have the sharp pains now if I'm careful how I move. Just a dull ache." She spoke slowly and in monotone. "I can breathe better." She touched her chest. "Whatever is in there has moved lower." Her weak-sounding voice halted after a few words, as if testing how her breathing was doing. "I needed that nap. Haven't slept much lately."

Woody thought of the many phone conversations when he'd ask, "How are you, Mom?" She'd reply, "Oh, fine," and they'd move on to another topic. She wasn't one to draw undue attention to herself. He'd have to keep in mind to pry further about her health.

Everyone in the room seemed pleased with the diagnosis, and Dr. Sloan said they'd know more in the morning about her remaining in the hospital or going home. He bade them good-bye and left the room.

"You go home, Woody," his mom said.

"I'll stay," he replied.

Although her voice was weak, his mom's eyes held censure. "I don't want you watching me sleep. And you need to take care of Sophie."

"She hates me," he said.

"She wouldn't if you didn't hate her."

"She's welcome to stay the night with us," Nancy said.

His mom closed her eyes for a moment. "That might be best. Woody will make her a nervous wreck."

Seeing Nancy's head turn toward him, he caught her quick glance and could almost read her mind that said Sophie was already a nervous wreck. He saw her grin, but she refocused on his mom.

Maybe he should ask for some of that miracle medication that helped one's breathing. He should not feel awkward, ill at ease. The only reason, he told himself, was that he didn't want Nancy to feel uncomfortable. She likely thought he'd be uncomfortable because she rejected him so many years ago.

But both had moved on. He wished there were some way they could be…probably not friends, but…comfortable.

And yet, the night Nancy had kissed him so thoroughly, declared her love, and he had not responded outwardly, only inwardly, he'd never been exactly comfortable with her again. He could not see her, think of her, hear her name, be close without being aware of how she changed from being a girl to a woman each time he saw her—the way she talked, what was in her gaze as she looked at him.

Now she looked away, hardly met his eyes at all. Or was

it he who feared he'd show…what? Regret? Yes, of course. Regret that he could only be friends with her family when she wasn't there.

They were mature now. He'd thought he was mature when in college, then in grad school, then while getting his doctorate. Now he realized just how young he'd been. Both were sensible now, aware they had not been meant for each other. In fact, no woman had been meant for him. Obviously.

His glance moved to the little snow globe on the bedside table. Had Nancy brought it in? She was wearing a white sweater. Did she remember the night so many years ago when she wore a white jacket?

Of course not.

He watched her stand. His gaze moved to her hand, holding his mom's hand. She still wore her wedding rings. That meant Ben remained in her heart and mind. What a ridiculous thought. Of course he did. Ben was her husband. The father of their child. Look how many years he remembered things best forgotten. Marriage and family was an even deeper bond. His and Nancy's bond had been friendship between two people until that warm kiss on that cold wintry night. If her lips had never touched his… But they had.

"I should go," she said.

Yes, he thought. Either she, or he, should go.

"And don't worry," she added. "We'll take care of Sophie."

"She doesn't sleep in her hair bow," his mom said, "but she needs it in first thing in the morning, before breakfast. But Jean knows that. Oh," she added, "thank you for the prayer. I can't imagine a better way to wake up."

"You're welcome."

Woody wondered for a moment what he should do. But of course, he knew. He followed Nancy from the room. "Thank you," he said. "For sitting with Mom. And praying for her."

"I was glad to. If there's anything I can do—"

"There is. I mean, your being a nurse. You understand all

this better than I. Maybe you could let me know if she needs a nurse when she goes home."

"A lot depends on how she is in the morning. But she's obviously already improving. The meds are working."

"Thank you. Um, sure you don't want me to get Sophie?"

Nancy laughed then. "More likely Sophie would get you."

"True," he agreed.

For an instant, it felt like old times.

It felt that way, too, later when he drove from the hospital and passed the Walker house, where no lights shone from the windows. He parked in the driveway and went inside his mother's home, even missing the obnoxious yapping of Sophie. He felt alone.

But he had a good, full life.

He told himself that all the time.

It was true.

His friend Jim had taken a different route. Through the years they visited after being apart for a number of years, or they called, or sent a Christmas card, and Woody would be reminded of two things. One, he was fortunate not to be tied down with the woes of family, finances, sickness, troubles. Two, he was unfortunate not to be tied down with the joys of…

But, he needed to stop thinking, make sure the thermostat was turned down for the night, and go into the room that had always been his, in which he still kept a few personal items and clothes in the closet.

Soon, he lay beneath the covers, in the dark, but seeing the sparkle of the ring on Nancy's finger.

Ben had been dead for quite a while. He wasn't sure how long. Over two years? Maybe Nancy had married again. Surely he would have heard that. He never asked about her except to say he supposed Nancy was doing well. Jim, or his mom, would report briefly what was happening in her life and that all was well. Nancy could have married again. In younger days, she was not the type to wait around ad infinitum.

Regardless, the rings on her finger meant that in her heart, anyway, she was married, even if to a memory.

He knew there was no need to try to stop the memories. They had a way of lingering, or resurfacing.

In the dark, with his eyes closed, he saw the wedding as if it were happening now.

Chapter 8

Twenty-three years earlier...Jim's wedding

Weddings had a strange effect on people, Woody told himself. Some laughed. Some cried. Some nodded. Some looked stoic. And some had strange images of becoming a groom themselves.

Standing in front of the church as Jim's best man, watching the bridesmaids walk down the aisle, Woody had the strangest thought, right after acknowledging what had become an increasing awareness: that Nancy had grown up. He'd known it, of course, but had tried to put it out of his mind. She'd just completed her freshman year at Towson University. She was a cheerleader, like she'd been in high school, and active in student affairs. That's what Jim had told him when he asked about the Walker family.

Several of Lauren's bridesmaids, dressed in sunshine yellow, advanced down the church aisle, but Woody had no idea how any of them looked. His gaze was glued to Nancy. She'd become so beautiful, with her dark hair falling to her shoulders in soft waves and the sparkle in her brown eyes dancing as if she were the bride.

Her gaze met his. He couldn't look away, and swallowed hard, becoming as nervous as Jim had been a short while ago in that back room when Woody straightened his friend's bow tie, patted him on the arm, and promised to hold him up if he started to fall over.

When Nancy reached the front of the church, just before she turned to take her place opposite the groomsmen, she gave Woody that million-dollar smile of hers and looked at him with incredible devotion.

The "Wedding March" sounded on the piano, and Woody's gaze shifted like everyone else's to watch the bride glide down the aisle. Woody imagined Nancy as a bride. Of all people, he imagined himself as the groom.

Even then, with the bright sunlight of a June day shining through the windowpanes, Woody remembered that snowy night, a year and a half earlier. He remembered the light in her eyes and her confession of love. Was he her first love? Her first real love?

He'd had what he called mature, serious relationships in college. The kisses had become passionate, intimate. But he'd never experienced anything so pure, so sweet, as the night when Nancy's kiss thawed his frozen lips…and warmed his heart.

He reminded himself, as he had many times over the years, *We're still friends.*

He felt her friendship later when Nancy approached him at the reception, after wedding pictures had been snapped.

She poked his ribs, making him jump and almost spill his punch. He looked around and saw the mischief in Nancy's eyes. "I've got the tin cans and rope," she said.

He grinned. "I have the shaving cream."

"Let's go. Elaine brought crepe paper."

"Great," Woody said. "You and Elaine sneak out. Jim asked to borrow my car for their getaway. But I know he just did that so I'd decorate my own car, then he'd laugh and take his."

She lifted her gaze to the ceiling and back. "Well, I guess Jim's not the sharpest knife in the drawer."

Woody laughed. "Excuse him. He's in love."

"Are you?"

Woody's laughter caught in his throat. Her question sounded serious. He straightened and glanced around the crowded room instead of at her. "Go on," he said as playfully as he could, "before Jim sees us and suspects something."

Why had she asked? Had she not gotten over the crush she'd had on him? Was she asking if he could love her? Was she asking if he was serious about another girl?

He'd tried to be.

He'd tried to avoid Nancy after that Christmas kiss, and that hadn't been difficult. He'd seen little of her since he'd begun his master's studies. He and Jim had roomed together in the dorm then both worked at a boys' camp during the summer to help with their own tuition. He'd seen Nancy a couple of times after her high school graduation. They'd talked briefly about their academic plans, and she'd given him her senior picture. She'd asked for one of him, but he'd never given her one.

He knew how she'd looked, and how she'd changed. A college girl did not look like a high school girl. He thought of last Christmas, six months ago, when he'd considered the invitation from his girlfriend, Monique, to go home with her during the holiday and meet her parents. She'd said, "Or, I could meet yours."

The closer the time came for a decision, the stronger he felt about returning to Silver City, where his heart was. Monique had looked at him for a long moment then lowered her gaze and studied the ground. She said she had to go, had plans to make.

He hadn't stopped her.

He wondered, what had stopped him?

Of course he knew. Other than being in no position to get serious with a woman, he'd had to ask himself if he wanted to spend his life with Monique. She was fun, smart, pretty. But the answer was no. He couldn't chance getting too serious. Not after all the work and sacrifice his dad made to give Woody a good education.

He had wanted to go home and see his friends. He went home, visited the Walkers, talked with Nancy when she walked out with him when he headed for home.

She again declared her love for him.

"I haven't met anyone I like more than you, Woody," she said. "I've never been in love with anyone but you."

He hated having to say it. But he had to. How could she know what she felt for him was true love if she'd never given herself a chance with anyone else? "Go out with friends. Get to know guys."

"Oh, Woody. I do know guys. And I don't want to date anyone else."

"Nancy, you're barely nineteen," he'd said. "I'm six years older than you. You're too young to make a commitment, and I'm in no position to consider such."

Now, six months later, there he was, without Monique, tying tin cans to Jim's back bumper. He laughed, watching Nancy, in her bridesmaid's dress, climb into the backseat of the car. She wrote "Just Married" with shaving cream across the back windshield. Of course it was backward from the outside and hard to read. She didn't stop with that but made hearts, arrows, X's, and O's all over the car while Elaine tied red, white, and blue crepe paper streamers to the radio antenna and side mirror.

She was a romantic. He a realist. Temptation to abandon the rules and have that youthful outlook that love conquers all crossed his heart. But his mind overruled when Jim and Lauren came out, ready to leave.

"Hey, I'm taking your car, remember?" Jim said.

"Sorry," Woody replied. "Out of gas."

The rice-laden, laughing couple got into the decorated car and with horn blaring and cans clanking drove away from the church.

"Are you next?" Nancy asked, standing on the sidewalk beside him, while others headed for their cars or went inside the church.

Woody smiled but kept his eyes on the straight and narrow road ahead as Jim's car pulled out of sight. What to say? *You're too young? I'm too old? What would my wife and I live on? My dad's dream is my future since emphysema could prevent his having one? I get money from my parents, have student loans, and work in the summers?* Jim's new bride had completed business school. She would continue working at her secretarial job at the boys' camp while Jim completed his master's studies in accounting.

"Can't afford it," Woody decided to say. "Besides, studying and working take up all my time. I've applied to assist a professor in the master's course to help with tuition. I won't have a wife support me while I finish school."

She sighed. "Have you given up on flying?"

In younger years, both he and Jim had talked of becoming airline pilots and seeing the world. "I'd still like to travel someday. But for now, teaching history is more practical."

"Do you always have to be practical?" With a shake of her pretty head, she added, "You're impossible."

"No, Nancy. I'm not. Our age difference and life's necessities make a lot of things impossible."

She exhaled heavily. "I should have been born first. I should have been Jim."

Woody tried to joke. "Nah. I'm not attracted to Jim."

Her eyes challenged him. "Are you attracted to me?"

That prompted him to exhale heavily. "If you're so inclined, ask me again in a few years. After you get your college degree."

She yanked on his tux sleeve. "And what am I supposed to do in the meantime?"

He said what he must. How could either of them know if what she felt for him was true love if she'd never given herself a chance with anyone else? Oh, he knew from family conversations and Jim that she went out with a group she called *friends*. The two of them had called each other friends, too. But he wanted no regrets when he married for a lifetime. "Go out, Nancy. Get to know guys. Enjoy your life. You're young."

"I'll be a sophomore in college this fall, and I'm over eighteen," she said. "That's called being a grown-up."

"I know you're nineteen, but that's still a teenager," he reminded her, and himself.

Weak moments and temptation could cause one to forget about future plans, education, career, responsibility, and excuse it away with words based on emotion. Were he younger, and not quite so sensible, he would like to be the white knight in shining armor to this lovely girl. One could become lost in romantic moments, but for lasting commitment he believed one had to prepare, be ready, be certain.

He couldn't ask her to quit school and work to support him while he continued his education. He couldn't expect her to give up her college years, independence, plans for her own future…for him.

Anyway, she was probably kidding. Likely, she'd gotten over that teenage crush she'd had on him. Her eyes challenged him, as they had when she was seventeen. But perhaps she was just trying out her flirtations on a friend with whom she felt…safe.

He took a deep breath and exhaled. "Now, I promised to help clean up the fellowship hall after the reception."

"Whaddaya know? We have something in common." She lifted her skirt to her ankles and raced up the church steps.

He followed.

On the landing, she stopped, turned toward him, and pulled his boutonniere from his lapel. "Don't let the other girls nab you. You're still the most handsome man I know." She spoke in a warning tone. "Be careful who you look at with those dreamy blue eyes of yours. Remember, you're waiting for me to become middle-aged." She lifted the yellow rosebud to her nose.

Woody shook his head and returned her smile then held the door open for her to enter the church. They walked together down the aisle, headed for the fellowship hall.

But for now, he knew what he had to do. He would return to his job at the summer camp. His master's thesis topic and outline had been approved, and he needed to work on that as much as possible.

He tried to be careful not to discourage Nancy, and at the same time, not to encourage her.

Sometimes, Nancy, I'm not careful enough. Sometimes, I look at you perhaps too closely. Will you forget me, or will you again ask me if I'm attracted to you...someday?

Someday, when we're both better prepared.

Chapter 9

If anything could waft around a crack or through the keyhole of a closed door it was the smell of bacon. Nancy awoke to that and smiled. She never cooked bacon anymore for herself. But her mom paid no attention to fat or calories and had no obvious health problems.

She lay for a while, remembering last night. After returning home she talked with her mom for a long time about the symptoms Marge had experienced but ignored.

"I must go to the hospital in the morning," her mom had said. "I can't allow my friend to be in there without going to see her. I'd never be able to live with myself."

Nancy understood. She would have regretted it had she not been with her husband during his recuperation from the first heart attack and then the fatal one.

She understood, too, that Woody was practical enough not to stay the night at the hospital. His mother wasn't in a life-or-death situation. She needed her rest and so did he. Marge Lawing would require more help from him when she returned home than while she was at the hospital surrounded by nurses and an on-call doctor.

After going to bed Nancy had seen the sweep of light across her front window and heard a car pass the house. Even as she told herself not to look, she disobeyed and padded to the side window. She lifted a slat of the blind in time to see the dark sports car turn into the driveway two houses down.

Her mouth opened in surprise. Surely that wasn't Woody's low, sleek sports car. She expected him to drive at least a medium-size, substantial car like a sensible professor would drive. He always was sensible. Too sensible for her. In his mature years had he become young at heart? When he switched off the engine and the inside car light flicked on, Nancy let go of the slat and returned to bed. She forced her thoughts away from the past, closed her eyes, and made herself pray for Marge and the hospital personnel. Having worked as a nurse, she'd become particularly aware of how much patients and families looked to them for healing and help.

She prayed for her mother, her brother, and his family. And especially Rebekah who was taking exams and making life-changing decisions.

The next thing she knew, the early-morning light seeped around the closed blinds. Hearing a yap, she thought she'd better rise and get her share of the bacon. It probably smelled as appetizing to Sophie as it did to her.

Wearing her warm pajamas, Nancy entered the kitchen, and sure enough, her mom was holding up a piece of bacon.

"Sit," her mom said to the dog who was about to shake her insides out.

Sophie sat and looked right cute in that position, dressed for the day by wearing a pink bow in her hair.

"Speak," and the dog yapped. Nancy's mom fed Sophie a small piece of bacon. "Now go watch TV. I don't want to make you sick."

Amazingly, the dog turned and sashayed out of the kitchen.

"How do you do that?" Nancy asked.

"It's all in the tone of voice." She looked smug then admitted, "I think we both heard one of Sophie's favorite commercials come on. It's that squealing pig." She laughed pleasantly. "There's coffee in the pot. Omelet on the way, just the way you like it."

That meant eggs, sharp cheddar cheese, diced apple, a touch of milk, and a few leafy greens tossed in. "You spoil me, Mom." Nancy headed for the coffeepot sitting on the countertop.

"No more than you spoil me when I visit you."

Nancy took creamer from the refrigerator and poured some into her cup. She wasn't sure how to approach the subject on her mind. She supposed the best way was to jump right in. Well, not jump. Maybe…stick her big toe in.

She returned the creamer to the refrigerator and sat in a chair at the table, facing her mom. "You ever get lonely, Mom?"

Her mother nibbled at a piece of bacon, looking thoughtful. She swallowed and then spoke softly. "Oh, it was hard at first, losing your dad. It takes a while to get used to being alone." She smiled. "But I stay busy, have friends. Being alone and lonely are two different things."

Nancy glanced away from her mom and down at her cup. "I wonder if I should move back home."

"You mean buy a house here?"

"Maybe." Glancing at the surprised look on her mother's face, Nancy decided this wasn't the time to say she might move in with her.

Her mom shook her head and stirred the ingredients she'd been adding to a green bowl. She spooned the mixture into the omelet maker's two compartments and closed the lid.

"Listen to me, Nancy," she said in a determined voice as she set the stove timer for eight minutes. "You don't need to think about taking care of me. I'm doing fine."

"If I were close we could do things together."

"You know I love it when we're together, Nancy." Her mom faced her. "But you're at loose ends right now. So don't make any hasty decisions."

"It's not hasty, Mom. I knew when I had to move out of the parsonage and into that garage apartment my life had drastically changed. And now Rebekah lives in a dorm. Everything's different. Maybe…maybe I should even move back with you. For a while."

Her mom stepped over and put her hands on the table, reminding Nancy of a humped-back cat ready to spring. "You mean we could grow old together?"

Nancy winced. Yes, there was something to a tone of voice. "That's one way of putting it." To keep from saying something that would reveal her uncertainty, she reached for a piece of bacon and took a bite.

"You're too young to grow old, Nancy."

She felt reprimanded. "It's not a matter of old. It's…my life has changed, and I guess you're right. I'm at loose ends. But if I stayed with you, I'd get fat." She lifted the piece of bacon and took another bite.

"Now, Nancy. What would Ben say in a case like this? Or what would you say to a woman who came to you for advice?"

Nancy shook her head. At least, she could enjoy the bacon. "It's different when it's someone else. Easier to be objective."

"Just think about it," her mom said, and fortunately the timer pinged.

Think about it.

Nancy did. But that didn't take long. It was in her mind and in her life. Just facts she'd pondered since she moved into the garage apartment and Rebekah moved into a dorm.

She watched her mom put the omelets on two plates and pour orange juice. She poured her own coffee, sat down, and said a blessing. Nancy's mind was on her mother saying, *"You're too young to grow old."*

No, those youngish days were gone forever. Where does one go, how does one get on with life when only forty-two years old and a widow? When a great love comes along maybe once in a lifetime and love had already come to her twice? One love she couldn't have, however. But Ben and she had over twenty years together and produced a wonderful daughter who spoke of marriage and the mission field. Nancy could not regret that life. But she would not have more. She would not love again.

Complain?

Yes, she could.

But she determined not to.

She'd heard laments, witnessed grief, and listened to tales of loneliness and even depression. She, being a pastor's wife, had been expected to have answers. She'd counseled widows and advised them to get involved with projects helping others. That's what Nancy's mom had done after she became a widow. She volunteered more at the hospital. She baked more cookies than ever.

Now, however, since Nancy had been without Ben for over two years, she knew that volunteering and baking filled the time. Sure, anyone could fill the time. But one could be as lonely in a crowd as when alone. Maybe more so, when you see families together, even in a hospital, or when you take those cookies to a single mom who has small children. You count your blessings. But you count theirs, too. They have family…with them.

So, Nancy decided she would defy the words of Thomas Wolfe who said, "You can't go home again."

She would. She did.

"Come live with us," Nancy had said to her mom many years ago. "Now that Dad's gone, you don't have to ramble around in that house alone."

"It's home," her mom had said. "I want to be in my house."

Nancy didn't have that same feeling. She'd lived in a lovely parsonage in Asheville, North Carolina, for ten years. Then after Ben died, the associate pastor was waiting until she moved out. But she'd been busy getting Rebekah into college. The church members were eager to help and ensure all went well. Nancy became the one being helped by the church instead of her being the one to assist them. One couple even offered their lovely garage apartment in an affluent neighborhood rent free. Wise women said to take her time in making major decisions about her personal life so soon after her loss. This served perfectly.

The tables had turned. Instead of being the giver, she was the receiver.

Ben had died on a bright summer day. In the afternoon while in the church office, preparing his Sunday sermon. Life had seemed perfect. Then suddenly, only Ben's life was perfect because he'd gone to his heavenly home. Nancy had been strong for Rebekah.

During the past year Rebekah had turned to her boyfriend, Don Daves. They talked of marriage and the mission field. Nancy determined not to discourage them with words of their being young.

"Don't you like your life in North Carolina?" her mom said, bringing Nancy's thoughts back to the present.

"Everything's different."

Her mom nodded. "As time passes, Nancy, you'll discover you still have the blessings of home and family and friends and work. This is still new to you. And you've told me how helpful the church members have been."

Nancy nodded. "It's not excessive grief. I know I can get on with my life. But…" She paused to taste the omelet before it grew cold and to think about what she'd say. Finally, she simply said it: "I don't know where to sit anymore."

Her mom's glance took in Nancy sitting in the kitchen chair, and her eyebrows lifted. "Sit?"

Nancy didn't know where to sit in church. When Ben first

began to preach, she sat in the front row, supportive, proud, encouraging, praying.

After Rebekah was born, she took her turns in the nursery, and when it wasn't her turn she looked for guests or members who didn't come often, wanting to make sure they were welcomed.

After Ben died she was not the welcoming agent. She had to let the new pastor's wife do that, take her place, be the one with the friendly smile, with the answers to any questions, the one others looked at as not just one of them, but as one who might be a little more spiritual than they.

"I mean, in church. On the pew with the older widows?"

She hadn't known where to sit, so she began to sit in the back row when Rebekah wasn't with her.

Nancy didn't really find it comforting when her mom made a rather trite-sounding statement, perhaps meaning a rocker, when she said, "The Lord has just the right place for you to sit."

Chapter 10

Nancy's mom began to talk about Marge again and in no time had finished her breakfast. She pushed away from the table. "I'd better get ready to go."

Nancy agreed. "I'll clean up." She thought she'd add, conditioning her mom, "We make a good team, now don't we?"

Her mom lifted her eyebrows. "We'll see. Your babysitting Sophie will be a real test."

"I could cook more bacon."

"Too much could make her sick. Marge doesn't let her have table food often. But this is different. She needs to feel at home and special."

That's how Nancy wanted to feel. She finished her breakfast and had another cup of coffee while reading the Silver City weekly newspaper. She wanted to become familiar with this small town again, just in case she moved back.

Soon, her mom returned to the kitchen, ready to go. "I'll call as soon as I know anything," she said as she walked out the back door.

Nancy got up and carried her dishes to the countertop. She looked out the window over the sink as her mom pulled out of the carport. Farther down, there was no sports car in the driveway. She wondered, did he cook his own breakfast, pick something up at a fast-food place on the way, eat at the hospital?

When he was a little boy, he turned his nose up at omelets, but he liked her mom's pancakes drowned in maple syrup. He was always the really good-looking friend of her brother. He never seemed to notice her very much, but she watched him and Jim in all they did. She'd had the feeling they thought her a nuisance. She'd admired him all her life, even when he didn't know she existed.

Shaking her head, she reached over to turn on the TV and found *Good Morning, America*. She wasn't exactly sure what the subject was, while she emptied the dishwasher of last night's dishes, but thought those people laughed a lot and the group of onlookers yelled a lot. She washed the breakfast dishes by hand.

After checking on Sophie, who seemed to be napping, Nancy went to her bedroom to make the bed and put everything in order. Just as she was deciding how to dress for the day, her cell phone rang.

Seeing the name, she answered. "Hi, Mom."

She was glad to hear her mom say that Mrs. Lawing would be released midmorning. "Woody is here. I told him we would take care of Marge, you being a nurse and all."

Nancy's saliva went down her windpipe at that. Of course she'd look in on Marge, but no way could she be comfortable in that house, with Woody there, and pretend—

But by the time she got her throat cleared and started to protest, her mom clarified the situation. "Woody has already contacted Carl about a nurse, and she will meet us there."

After they rang off, Nancy found a rerun of *Best Dog in Show* on TV. Sophie responded, growled at some dogs, was silent with others, turned her back on still others, and gaped at a handsome male poodle. That reminded Nancy that some females longed for what simply was in their dreams only.

Nancy had always been more a cat lover. She thought of the one in North Carolina. When she and Rebekah moved out of the parsonage into the garage apartment, the landlords had mentioned they'd adored the cat. So when Rebekah decided to live in the dorm, she'd said Nancy could give the cat to the couple if she didn't want to take care of it herself.

Nancy's immediate thought was, *But I have no one else.*

She then reprimanded herself. She had…everything, and many people who cared about her, and she them. But in the end, she hadn't given away the cat, although her landlords were taking care of her while Nancy was away.

"Ah," she breathed when the phone rang again and Rebekah's name appeared. "Good morning, darling. How's it going?"

Rebekah shared that she felt good about yesterday's exams and was now at Starbucks having a mocha with Don. That should prepare her for the next two exams.

Nancy didn't bother to state that if she wasn't prepared, a mocha wouldn't do it.

"One more tomorrow and it's over," Rebekah said. "Then off we go to Honduras."

Nancy knew Rebekah's heart was in mission work. Now the passion was in her voice, and Nancy could almost see the sparkle in her daughter's eyes. They soon rang off after their words of love and Rebekah's promise to call when she had time.

Nancy smiled, thinking of the time when Rebekah took up most of hers. Even now, Rebekah was never far from her thoughts. While taking her shower, Nancy thought about Rebekah's life. She and Ben had given her a good one. But Rebekah also had her times of trials. She'd had the usual childhood diseases, hurts, disappointments, lost her grandfather at a young age, left her friends in Kentucky when Ben got a pastorate in North Carolina ten years ago. She'd had a teenage friend die in an automobile accident. Another had become addicted to drugs.

It wasn't that Rebekah had a rosy life, but she had Ben's nature, a gentle nature. She felt deeply and loved deeply. Her contentment came from reaching out to others.

That's what had appealed to Rebekah about Don. He'd wanted to be a missionary from an early age. Perhaps that came from his own upbringing. His mom and dad had been missionary journeymen when they were young. His dad now taught English at the Christian college Don attended, and his dad led the short missionary trips to other countries.

That reminded Nancy of Woody leading trips abroad. His were academically based, though.

She forced her thoughts back to Rebekah and Don, convincing herself again that they were not too young to know their own hearts and minds.

Don's mom was an area librarian and taught Bible studies at church. Dr. and Mrs. Daves loved Rebekah from the moment they met her. Nancy couldn't help but compare that with how the Walkers and the Lawings had related so well when their children were young. Although geography separated them for years, a bond remained.

She didn't know how she might get across the barrier of Woody's rejection to a comfortable friendship again. Perhaps that was impossible.

How could she relate to a man she didn't know really well, when she remembered so well the boy, and the young man whom she had loved?

Some things, she was thinking as she stepped from the shower and towel-dried, just had to be let go.

She dressed casually. Brown denims, chunky heels, cream-colored, cotton-knit top.

Her mom called again shortly after eleven o'clock.

"I just pulled into the Lawing driveway. Woody and the nurse are getting Marge out of the car. I'll stay a little while."

"I can bring Sophie down."

"Wait awhile. We wouldn't want Sophie jumping all over Marge just yet."

Nancy put on her jacket, and Sophie seemed eager when she snapped the hook of the leash onto her collar. She took her to the backyard and told her to go behind the bushes, but Sophie wanted to water the nandina shrub whose green leaves had turned red for the winter. They looked beautiful for Christmas in particular. No telling what Sophie's watering might do, however.

Sophie finished and marched herself to the back door. Nancy followed.

As soon as she came in Sophie ran to the front door and threatened it with her barking.

Now, who could that be?

At the same time the thought came…she knew exactly who that would be. And it wouldn't be Jean Walker.

Well, good. She'd simply hand the leash to him and be done with it. But, what if their hands touched? *Oh, for goodness' sake, Nancy, grow up!*

Chapter 11

Woody heard Sophie's shrill barking the moment he stepped onto the Walkers' first step. He paused at the door. All he needed to say was, "I've come for the mutt." But saying that in front of Sophie might be dangerous.

And Nancy might like the dog. She'd favored cats when she was young. Yet she'd changed her mind about what, or rather who she liked when she was young. He didn't really know her now. But last night, she seemed the same. Or maybe it's just that he remembered her the way she was when he did know her.

He needed to stop that train of thought, so he rang the doorbell.

She opened the wooden door. Seeing she held the leash, he opened the screen door. Sophie barked a warning.

"Looks like she doesn't like you either," Nancy said.

"Temperamental," he said. "She acts like she's going to attack me every time. After a while she settles down and tolerates me though. She's really the proverbial more bark than bite."

"I'm not convinced," Nancy said, and she laughed.

Her face was beautiful, a little flushed and surrounded by her dark wavy hair almost to her shoulders. She was wearing a jacket. "Were you going to bring Sophie home?"

"No, we just had an appointment out back."

Ah, that would account for her pink cheeks. "I see. Well, I suppose she's ready to go. I'll have to walk her. Two carloads of women are there, bearing food." He hiked his thumb toward his mom's house. "I'm not about to go into that house just yet." He glanced at her jacket. "Since you're dressed for it, would you like to walk with us?"

She didn't answer immediately, so he added, "But if you're busy—"

"No, I'm not." She handed him the leash, stepped out, and closed the door behind her.

Sophie pulled. "Not yet," he said to the dog, "not with a houseful of women in there."

They walked past his mom's house, and Sophie settled down to sniffing every bush and brick, marked her territory, then pranced like she owned the neighborhood. They talked briefly about who used to live in which house. Some old neighbors still did, others were gone.

There were a few children in the playground at the end of the street, so at the corner they turned. "I want you to know," she said, "I can check on your mom anytime. And you know my mom will. I suppose you have to get back to school."

"It's exam time," he said. "Everything's scheduled already. I'll see how Mom does today and tomorrow. The nurse is a day nurse. And I don't know about leaving Mom alone at night. Depends on how she gets along this weekend. I don't have to get back to the college, but I could during the day and come home at night."

They walked on around the block and up the next street.

"The Dobbins still live there," he said as they passed their house.

"Mom said Clara's niece married one of the Knight boys," Nancy said. "She said he painted the homeless."

"Yes, Thomas Knight. He was in my history class. I attended his debut art exhibit."

Her smile lit her face in delight. "Mom told me about it. Said it was all the news in Silver City. Local boy makes good sort of thing."

Woody nodded. He told her about Thomas living like a homeless man so he could paint the homeless with truth and honesty. "He's an example of one who really uses his life and talent to make a difference in the world." He took a deep breath. "As you have, Nancy. I'm sure your being a nurse and a pastor's wife has been a blessing to many."

She nodded. "My kind of personality needed to be where I saw the needs of others, where I was forced, or rather challenged, to think of them instead of myself. It's good to be mature enough to look back and see how God works in a life."

"True," he said. "We can't see ahead. And so often we think we know what's best for us. Or, we want what we want, regardless."

She looked over and up at him for a moment then said quietly, "You always seemed to make mature, intelligent decisions."

"I tried."

"Neither you nor Jim became pilots," Nancy said reflectively. "Why not?"

Woody thought for a moment. He could look back on his life and analyze it better than when he'd been younger and looked ahead. "My dad thought it more practical, a more secure future, for me to be a teacher. His goal in life was to work and save and send me to college so I wouldn't have to work except during the summer. My becoming Dr. Lawing was his goal, and it became mine." He smiled over at her.

"Now he isn't even here to see me use that doctorate, or hear me talk about my profession."

"You fly now." She smiled, a small twinkle in her eye.

"I am flown. When I first began taking college students to Europe, to see the places I teach about, I thought about the pilot. I thought I had an easier position sitting as a traveler than having the responsibility of all those passengers." He returned her smile. "But I soon discovered that keeping track of twenty or so college students wasn't exactly the easier situation."

"I guess not," she said. "You love it, don't you?"

"I—"

He felt his breath quicken. Yes, he'd said "I do" to academics, to a future, to college students instead of to Nancy. He'd made his choices. He'd like to say something to let Nancy know if he knew then what he knew now, his "I do" might have been different.

"I do, but—" His sentence stopped when three women stepped from the porch of his mom's house. Two went to a car, and Jean Walker hurried toward him and Nancy. Or to the dog, rather. "Oh, here's Sophie. Marge is eager to see her." She looked at Nancy. "You didn't bring her food and bed, did you?"

"Oh, I didn't yet. We were just walking her. I'll go get them."

"Sophie and I will," Woody said and glanced toward the car with the two women now in it.

"All right," Nancy said, understanding.

When they arrived at her house, she didn't invite him in. How different than when they were young. Then, he might simply knock and turn the knob and peek in, calling out for Jim. But after that night beneath the maple tree, everything changed. He became too aware of Nancy, always remembering the touch of her lips on his, his on hers. He became too aware of how she looked, the fragrance of her hair, the young girl becoming a woman, a very desirable woman.

He'd known not to sit beside her when he visited. So now, he wouldn't step inside, but he stood outside the door waiting for her to bring the dog food and the dog bed.

His gaze moved to the porch swing. He stared for a long moment. Then he heard the screen door open, and he quickly looked away from the swing, the last place where he'd sat beside Nancy.

No, this looked like a different swing. But the chaos within him was the same. He'd had choices. He'd made them. How could he know what was in the best interest of another, or even himself? He'd often pondered whether he'd been noble, or selfish.

With the leash wrapped around his left hand, he reached for the bag she held out to him. Sophie was circling his ankles with the leash. Woody struggled to keep the bag from dragging on the ground.

"Sure you don't want some help?" Nancy said.

He turned in circles to get untangled. He hoisted the bag up and secured it against his side with his upper arm. "No, I've got it."

Sophie was pulling to the walkway. Nancy was closing the screen door.

He was still saying no to Nancy.

And what might have been, had passed him by.

He didn't need to look at the swing to his right, or the maple tree to his left. So long ago Nancy had the door to her heart open. He never walked through. Now she was closing the door. He'd said no too many times, and she'd stopped loving him a long time ago.

And now, he was being pulled along while holding a garbage bag filled with a dog's paraphernalia.

To make it worse, the dog didn't even like him.

Chapter 12

Nancy closed the screen door and watched for a moment. In earlier years she would have laughed about Woody standing there with a dog leash wrapped around his ankles.

But this was Dr. Lawing, looking uncomfortable, being handed a garbage bag.

During those earlier years she'd seen what she wanted to see. In those days she believed there would be a happy ending to her life. *Well*, she thought, as she closed the wooden door, *there had been. With Ben.*

For a moment she stood with her back against the door and looked at the living room. Her mom had replaced the furnishings, but these were just as inviting, cozy, and comfortable. Nancy could be happy here. But she got the feeling her mom might not want her here.

She walked into her bedroom. Maybe she should peek out and make sure Sophie hadn't tried the ankle and leash trick again, causing Woody to be sprawled on the sidewalk.

Looking through the blind, she saw Sophie tugging and

Woody walking briskly. She supposed, with a tad of resentment, the college students kept him young.

Just as she thought of turning to remove her jacket, her eyes lit upon the porch swing. That was the last place she'd ever sat beside Woody. Oh, how long ago? About twenty years, she supposed.

Twenty-three years earlier...

In one sense, time crawled between the times Nancy saw Woody. In another sense, time flew. She loved college. Becoming a sophomore at Towson was more fun than the freshman year. She began to see the wisdom of finishing one's education before entering another phase of life. After driving almost an hour to and from the university each day, staying for Christian Student Group meetings, being involved in CSG projects, going to games and cheering, not to mention studying, she hardly had time to breathe...except for doing what Woody had suggested—going out with friends and having a good time. That was her favorite subject.

She always looked to see if Woody's car was in the driveway. She knew it wouldn't be, but she couldn't resist looking and hoping just to catch a glimpse. She also smiled at the maple tree and remembered Woody's kiss.

Listening to Jim and Lauren, she began to understand the wisdom of waiting until after completing one's education before getting married. Although they loved each other, their lives weren't filled with being in each other's arms day and night. In fact, they complained that they'd seen each other more before getting married.

It was a year after Jim's wedding before Nancy talked with Woody again, on a personal level. He always sent her a birthday card in July. He would know she would soon turn twenty, no longer a teenager. Surely he would now consider her a woman. He was twenty-six, but they were both adults.

He could get a teaching job; she could get nurses' training almost anywhere.

When she came home from her summer job at the hospital, her heart leaped. Woody stood leaned up against the maple tree—the symbol of her declaration of love. He looked even more handsome and mature each time she saw him. He stepped out of the shade and into the sunshine toward the car as she pulled into the driveway.

She literally ran to meet Woody. Surely his own heartbeat matched hers as she laid her head against his chest. She felt his chin against the top of her head, then he moved back. She wished for a kiss, but he had something else on his mind.

After she gushed out her greetings and how glad she was to see him and asked how was everything and did he get his master's, he laughed.

"Whoa!" He held up a hand to stop her questions that were running together. But so were her emotions. She doubted this was the way an adult should behave. But she was just so glad to see him. His being here meant…something!

"Could we talk?" he asked.

Oh my, if he were going to propose, she didn't want it to be with her in the clothes she'd worked in at the hospital all day. "Let me run in for a minute. Be right back."

"I'll sit in the swing," he said.

Nancy ran inside, quickly freshened herself, put on a skirt and sleeveless blouse. She took her hair out of its pins and brushed it out down to her shoulders. Golden flecks of merriment danced in the brown eyes looking at her from the mirror.

She applied lipstick, took off the rubber-soled shoes and slipped into sandals, and dabbed on a tad of Beautiful perfume. Now she looked more like a woman ready for a commitment from a man who wore slacks and a short-sleeved sport shirt.

Woody's glance swept over her when she walked out onto the porch. "You look…nice," he said, but his expression didn't match what she was feeling. He patted the space beside him on the swing.

Nancy didn't think he would be reticent about proposing. He was neither an introvert nor a shy person, just…obstinate and stubborn. She sat and clasped her hands on her lap, bracing herself for whatever he might say. Maybe he'd found someone else. How could she stand it? How could she possibly act like an adult if he said something ridiculous like that?

She heard his intake of breath, then his exhale. That meant he felt some kind of uncertainty. She was reluctant to take a breath at all. Then he spoke.

"Nancy, to answer your questions, everything's fine with me. Is it…with you?"

Nancy darted a glance at him, saw distress on his face, and looked out at the yard, but not the maple tree. "I've finished my sophomore year," she said. "And like always, I'm working during the summer at the hospital." She shrugged. Those things were insignificant. *What's going on with us?* She wanted to scream, *I'm not a patient person.*

"Nancy," he said.

She nodded, as if having to acknowledge that she was Nancy. If he said something awful, she would be nobody… nothing…mud!

"My master's thesis turned out better than I expected. I've been granted a scholarship to study in Europe and expand on the thesis for my doctorate."

Nancy felt numb. The doctorate part didn't surprise her. She knew he wanted to teach history on a college level. But… Europe? She managed to choke out that word. "Europe?"

Nancy couldn't believe it. Surely she'd heard him wrong. "Tell me you didn't say that."

"For at least a year."

She had to know. He already knew she was in love with him. She couldn't be any more blunt about it than she already had. So, why not make a fool of herself again? "Are you asking me to go with you?"

When he didn't answer immediately and she saw the struggle in his expression, she figured he was trying to spare her feelings. But if he didn't love her, there was no sparing of them. Finally, he spoke. "I won't have time for anything but studies, Nancy."

"I could work. I mean, can't you just see us flying off to Europe together? You always talked about flying."

He shook his head. "Nancy, please. I can't do that. You couldn't make enough money there to meet expenses. And I'm not going to have any free time."

She was not one to give up. "Are you asking me to wait for you?"

He shut his eyes then, but not before she saw the pained expression in them. She knew the answer before he said it. Finally he opened his eyes. "In all fairness to you, I won't ask that. You need to prepare for your future. You're still very young."

"I'll wait for you, Woody. I still love you."

"Don't put your life on hold for me. You're going to fall head over heels with some guy other than me. It's just that you've known me all of your life."

She was shaking her head before he finished the sentence. "No, Woody. I've known a lot of guys all my life. I love *you*. I always will."

He stood. "Whatever my feelings for you, I can't talk to you about this. I'll be in Europe for at least a year. That will occupy all my time and energy. I can't promise you anything. I'm headed for thirty years old. I have to prepare to make my own way. I can't live off my parents then a wife till I'm middle-aged."

"Why not?"

"Because I try to be reasonable and responsible. And I don't want you to put your life on hold for something we haven't even fully discussed. Go out, have fun in the short while you'll have between studying and working."

"Is that what you're going to do?"

"This is going to be even more demanding than my master's. But if I have any free time, yes I expect to sightsee, go out with friends." The sun seemed to have gone behind a cloud and shadowed his face. His voice was subdued, and she didn't really believe he meant what he was saying. "Nancy, we haven't made any commitment to each other. I cannot in all good conscience do that. You understand?"

She understood and respected him for his dedication to his dad, to his studies, to his future. But she also understood her heart and mind. "Will you kiss me good-bye?"

He took her by the shoulders, and she was afraid he might kiss her cheek. She put both her hands on his face and lifted her face to his. His arms went around her, and she felt herself melt into them, against his chest.

Surely, only one heart couldn't beat that strongly. He had to feel it, too. Their hearts beating together. All right. She would understand. He wasn't rejecting her. He was saying wait.

His face was so close, bending toward hers. She watched his lips. "Nancy," he breathed, his mouth so close to hers she felt his breath, and she was sure he was about to declare his love and even say he couldn't leave without her. His lips touched hers. Moved against hers. Everything else faded.

But then he moved her away. His words were not of love. He stepped back. "There's Jim's car."

She turned her head to see Jim and Lauren drive up. Woody made a hasty departure down the steps and toward the car. Was he more eager to see them than— No! It's just that he would think Jim wouldn't approve of anything going on between his little sister and Woody.

He was sensible.

So she followed, to greet her relatives and pretend.

But she would wait.

Wait, so they could enjoy each other and life on a more cheerful basis than Jim and Lauren. They would have time for each other. They would not have to worry about making ends meet.

Of course he was right.

And hadn't she told herself a long time ago… True love can wait.

Chapter 13

"Have you ever seen such generous people?" Woody's mom said after the two ladies from church came in with breakfast, still warm from being in tightly closed dishes and wrapped in foil.

"Well, yes," he answered. "Even when I was a boy, you and Mrs. Walker often left home with boxes of food for others. It's not one-sided."

"That's a wonderful thing about living right here in this small town. As much as I love you, these people are my family."

He looked at the note the ladies left on the countertop, letting them know who would bring lunch, dinner, and breakfast the following morning.

"Looks like I'm not needed," he said while filling his plate.

His mom filled hers and sat at the table while he poured coffee for both. She made a tsking sound. "Oh, we need each other," she said.

He pointed his fork at her. "You don't want me to think you need me."

"Oh, we do." A very serious expression crossed her face. "We're family."

He already knew that but took a bite, waiting to hear what was on her mind.

"I guess it's that bond that we always need and go back to. Did you know Nancy might move back here?" she asked him.

That surprised Woody. He thought of Nancy as being gone forever. She was only visiting for Christmas.

His mom looked across at him and must have detected his surprise. She nodded. "She's talking about moving in with Jean. But Jean's like me. We want our independence as long as we can have it." She chewed a bite and swallowed. "Like you, I guess. You obviously like living alone."

Woody knew her statement was really a question. One that had been thoroughly discussed through the years. He reached out and stabbed another piece of sausage. "Good cooks, those women."

"Sausage is sausage," she said and reached down to give a small bite to Sophie who waited at her feet.

He didn't want to hear what he knew was in his mom's mind. Nancy was lonely— His thoughts stopped when his mom said, "Oops," as she straightened and put her hand to her chest. "I'm okay. Doesn't really hurt, but when I move a certain way, I feel it like it's a knot or something." She lifted a consoling hand. "Much better than yesterday, I can tell you that."

Then the discussion moved more to Christmas. "I should have this house decorated by now," she said. "Jean and I were talking about it. Oh, she wants a real tree this year since her family is coming here." She grew thoughtful for a moment. "Now don't get offended, Woody. But I don't think I should go away this Christmas. Maybe I'll have a real tree for a change, too."

"I'm glad you said that, Mom. Carl indicated you need to take it easy for quite a while. You don't want a relapse."

She smiled and looked beyond him, wearing a reminiscent expression. "Jean and I used to talk about the ornaments, the decorations, after our husbands died and our children were gone. In the past few years I've gone to wonderful places with you for Christmas, and Jean went to Jim's or Nancy's. This year we're going to stay home and decorate real trees." She looked at him then, as if to say *"Guess who's been elected to get them and set them up?"*

"We can see about that," he said. "When would you two like to go?"

"I'll call her," she said. "But, don't you need to get back to Georgetown?"

The drive was not much over half an hour. His grading of the exams could wait, but he'd like to get that out of the way and have a couple of weeks free. And he worked best in the place where he…obviously liked.

"I would like to go back for a couple days," he said, "but only if the nurse can stay the night with you."

She shrugged. "Or someone from church. There are other old ladies just like me. And they like this big TV you got me. We can actually see the actors."

He laughed at her humorous way of accepting getting older. The nurse came before they finished breakfast and went to straighten his mom's bedroom. His mom asked him to pour her another cup of coffee and hand her the landline phone that sat on the countertop.

Knowing she'd be calling someone to spend the night, he went into his bedroom to see what he might take with him to Georgetown. His gaze lit upon the little snow globe on the end table.

Yesterday, when they were ready to leave the hospital, his mom had wrapped it in a plastic bag and put it in her purse. Later in the day she'd taken it out and handed it to him.

"You could put it on your night table," she said. "I have that big one I put in my room that your dad gave me a long time ago. It plays music, and the snow dances around."

This one did not play music. He remembered looking at it and praying his mom would be all right. He also remembered Nancy's hand that had set it on the table by the hospital bed.

He would leave it here. It didn't really fit with his Georgetown lifestyle.

Soon, his mom informed him that a widowed friend looked forward to coming over. She wanted to see *An Affair to Remember*. He knew that was one of his mom's favorite movies. Women in their seventies watching it. Did remembering never end? He knew the answer. In many ways he grew older. In some ways, and at times, he felt like just a little boy needing his mama, a young man needing his dad, a maturing man—

There was something he must do.

Stop behaving like a man rejected and making his lifelong friend feel uncomfortable. Her family, his friends, were coming for Christmas. They needed to relate. He needed to try to be as kind and thoughtful as his mom and her friends, and that included Jean Walker and Nancy.

He heard Sophie at the back door. He might take her for a walk and stop by the Walkers. No. If he was going to be a man about this, he shouldn't lean on a dog or make that his excuse as if he just happened by. Sophie pulled with her teeth at the leash hanging on the back door. Woody ignored her and opened the door so she could run outside. He closed the door against the wind that felt colder than yesterday.

However, he decided not to drive to the Walkers. Nor call.

Soon, he was ringing the doorbell.

Nancy came to the door. "Is your mom all right?" was the first thing she said, after drawing a surprised breath. Or perhaps it was just a cold, windy breath.

"Fine. Yes. I wonder, Nancy. Would you like to go with me for a cup of coffee or something? Downtown?"

He'd rather ask her out to one of the excellent restaurants in DC like Sequoia, or the fun ones like Tony & Joe's, where they could laugh and sample various foods, but he didn't want this to look like…something it wasn't. And he had no idea what that thought meant.

But he managed to say, "I owe you an apology."

Chapter 14

Nancy heard a movement behind her and knew her mom had come into the living room. She walked up to them. "Woody," she said, "is Marge all right?"

He gave a brief report, assuring her all was well.

"Would you like to come in? Have coffee? I'm baking cookies. I'll take some down to Marge in a little while."

"No, thank you. I'll be driving back to Georgetown before long. I intend to get things settled at the university, then I'm available for"—he spread his hands—"bringing home Christmas trees and getting them set up."

"Oh, so she talked to you about that. Good."

"I'll be back in a couple days or so."

"Wonderful."

Her mom gave a little wave and retreated.

Nancy had been staring, studying how he looked. His handsome face had cheeks touched by the cold. His blue eyes shone bright. The gray at his temples enhanced the waves tossed to and fro around his head.

She didn't know if downtown meant DC or Silver City. As if it mattered.

And he owed her an apology?

The only thing she could think of that he'd ever done wrong was reject her. That wasn't exactly like jilting one at the altar. After all, he'd never promised anything. He'd liked her more than just as a friend, whatever that meant.

All right. Suppose he apologized for rejecting her.

Would that fix the years? The memories?

Was he sorry he hurt her?

Was he sorry he missed out on having a life with her?

He didn't look sorry. He looked…as wonderful as ever.

Would he apologize for not falling in love with her? If that's what people did, she'd have to apologize to about six billion of them.

The offer was a cup of coffee, or something, with an apology?

Long ago, she would take whatever little crumb he might toss her way. She could at least listen to his apology now. And what would she say? That's all right. I stopped loving you when Ben came along? Just turned it off like a water faucet? Watched it go down the drain like bathwater? Or a little more slowly like a snow melting away after a cold winter? Or even more slowly like a wound that leaves a scar that eventually is almost, almost faded away…

"You don't mean walk?"

He grinned. "This time of year, it's mainly the treadmill for me. But not a dozen miles or so."

So, the dozen miles must mean Silver City.

He said, "I can get my car."

She nodded. Wouldn't want to appear too anxious. "Give me five minutes?" She'd already dressed for the possibility of going with her mom to see…Marge.

After a quick bathroom trip, applying fresh lip gloss, and donning her jacket over the denims and blue sweater, she went to the kitchen door. "Mom, I'll be back in a little while. I have my phone."

She didn't wait to hear a question or a comment, but turned to go. Following her up the hall were her mom's words. "No hurry."

Well no. She was in no hurry. Just because it was a few seconds before five minutes didn't mean a thing. She walked out onto the porch as Woody drove up. He opened the driver's door but closed it when he saw her. He reached over to turn the handle of the passenger side.

Nancy got in and closed the door. The inside was warm. He must have started the motor right away. The interior smelled like leather and him. One Christmas she'd given him a bottle of the musky aftershave that Jim said he used.

Now, it seemed almost overpowering. Not the scent but the memories, and now sitting in this sleek sports car, the dark interior seeming like a world of its own, with the outside world blocked out. The low, plush seats of black leather, the intimacy of being so close.

What am I doing, she wondered, *making new memories in this dark cocoon of comfort and luxury? I can't go back. I can't go forward. Once you've been rejected...*

"Smooth," she said and glanced around the interior while touching the air bag section in front of her.

He looked over at her and grinned. "Makes the young people envious, and maybe they'll think I'm not such an old fogey."

"I doubt they think that." Then she decided to ask, "What do you think. About them?"

His glance at her before returning to the road indicated he wasn't sure what she was asking.

"You like teaching college-age students?"

"Not only is it my profession," he said, "it's my mission."

She was about to ask him to elaborate but light sparked

his blue eyes. "You know, I met Rebekah a few times." He sounded pleased. "She's a lovely girl."

Yes, she knew he'd met Rebekah at Jim's in Virginia.

That led to conversation about Rebekah being between the ages of Jim and Lauren's children, Stephen and Carol, both of whom were now in college but would come home for Christmas.

He drove past the Knight Hotel, looking inviting with its white lights outlining the three-story building, welcoming those who might come in from under the cloud-laden sky.

"I don't believe this was here when we were young." He pulled into the parking lot at the side of The Silver Percolator.

"The town's built up more. Some businesses closed. Others came in."

"Jim and I have been here a few times." He switched off the engine, and she opened her door. He got out, shut his door, and touched the remote, causing the lights to blink.

Inside the café, she said, "Glenda and I came here a few years ago. The word is, it's the best coffee place in town."

"The only, I believe. Where would you like to sit?"

The irony of his question made her laugh and shake her head.

He smiled as if thinking it didn't really matter. "What about that booth by the window?"

"Has a great view." She glanced toward the black sports car near the window.

"Then, by all means." He spread his hand toward the booth, and they walked to it and slipped in opposite each other.

"Just coffee," she said when the waitress came.

"Cream?" he said, and she nodded. He remembered? She'd begun drinking coffee with cream when she was seventeen, not because she liked it, but because that's what grown-ups did. Then, she'd acquired the habit.

He took his with cream, too.

The conversation was general. The weather turning colder,

although neither mentioned snow. When Jim and his family would come.

Woody said it's amazing how people can live near each other but rarely visit. "Our lifestyles are different, but our friendship remains."

The coffee came.

She took a sip. Whether it was good didn't matter. It was coffee. She set the cup down and held her hands on her lap. "You wanted to apologize?"

He nodded, staring at his coffee cup. Then he looked across at her with a serious face and eyes deep with meaning.

"I saw you at the hospital, and again yesterday when Sophie led us down the sidewalk." He did smile then, and she returned it. "I didn't ask about you, Nancy. I mean personally. I was concerned about Mom and—"

"Of course you were." What did he mean?

He took a deep breath and gave a slight shake of his head. "I know we've both lost our dads. And…others. But," he said, "I really can't imagine what it's like losing someone like you have. Mom has. Your mom has. I should have said something."

Nancy felt relief. At least he hadn't apologized for not loving her. For rejecting her. For breaking her heart.

"No, it really wasn't the time," she assured him. "There, with all the people around, I'd just say I'm fine. This way, I can say more."

He wasn't drinking his coffee. Did he feel as clumsy as she? Surely not. He was always so…controlled.

She wrapped both hands around her cup. "I really am fine about Ben's death. We knew about his weak heart and that it could happen. Of course, you're never prepared, regardless."

He nodded, and she remembered how concerned he'd been in the hospital about his mom. He'd lost his dad. And hers. She wanted to reach over and take his hands. But she couldn't.

She smiled at her cup for a moment. Yes, coffee served its

purpose. "It was, and I suppose always will be in a way, difficult for me and especially for Rebekah, her being so young."

Seeing the tender look in his eyes spurred her on. He had asked. She would tell him. "I can handle Ben's being in heaven. I mean, death is something I have no control over. Those things I have to turn over to God and let Him handle it." She chuffed. "But having to climb a ladder. That bothers me. Heights, you know. But it doesn't bother me to be in an airplane. That, too, is so much out of my control, I give it to God."

"Yes," he said so seriously she wanted to ask if he really knew that. What in his life had he given to God? She wanted to know this man. The real Woodrow Lawing.

He chuckled. "That's rather how mom talks. She says others joke about a woman having to change lightbulbs, but it's really one of the most aggravating, difficult things to do."

Nancy nodded. "So true. And I never know my tires are low on air until someone tells me." She picked up her cup and took a sip then made a face.

The waitress stepped over from the next booth. "Is your coffee all right?"

"Cold," she said. "Not your fault. I just haven't been drinking it."

"I'll get more," she said.

Woody set his over, too.

"But you'll never believe what bothers me most of all."

His eyes widened. His dark eyebrows lifted.

Nancy leaned forward. "It's why I laughed when you asked where I wanted to sit. I had that conversation with Mom recently."

She leaned back because the waitress brought the coffee. She wondered if he leaned away from her inane comments.

They both sipped the hot coffee and nodded at the waitress who waited to see if they were pleased. "Perfect," he said.

"You see," she began again. "Where to sit is within my control. And it makes me want to stop going to church."

He laughed then apologized. "Sorry."

She thought this was a lot like old times. She'd say something ridiculous and make him laugh. "I know it's silly. But it's real. When I was a pastor's wife I didn't even mind sitting alone, or with those I didn't know. I had a position."

Since he was listening while drinking his coffee, she continued, telling him about her feelings about sitting in the back row, or with widows. "Isn't that silly?"

The wrinkle on his brow indicated he was thinking about that, so she sipped her now warm coffee. After a moment, he set his cup down and spoke as if this were the most serious conversation in the world. "I suppose I've sat alone so much it doesn't bother me. The college-age girls and boys don't sit with me unless there's some special occasion in which we go together and there are other adult chaperones. I usually find a seat near the back or near the aisle, but it doesn't matter." He studied her for a moment. "I think it might be a girl thing?"

"Possibly. We girls are more emotional, more inclined to seek companionship."

"Or," he said, "maybe boys seek companionship in different ways than girls. Like…hanging out at ball games." His eyes twinkled. "While the girls keep us supplied with chips, chicken wings, and drinks to wash them down."

Nancy, suppressing a chuckle, finished her coffee and set the cup aside. She shook her head, just as he did, when the waitress started to come over.

"Of course," Woody continued, "that doesn't happen often. Maybe during the World Series when four or five single guys come over."

"And the girls keep you supplied with food," she said, nodding. She then raised an eyebrow in mock challenge.

"You know me better than that…" He paused, smiled a little, then grew serious again. More distant. "But the old single guys, of whom I'm the youngest, and the divorced one who doesn't have a girlfriend at the moment, get together occasionally."

That really didn't tell her much. But then, he never really *had* told her much. She smiled. "When you're not out of the country."

"Right. But that's mainly during the summer."

She couldn't help but ask and tried to keep her voice moderate, "You have an exciting life, don't you?"

His quick glance told her nothing. But pulling the billfold out of his jacket pocket he said, "A fulfilled one." He laid a bill on the table then looked across at her seriously. "But like you, when it's out of my control, I turn it over to God." He scoffed lightly. "That tends to be the story of my life. Ready?"

She'd rather hear the story of his life. But what more should one say about a fulfilled life?

On the way home they talked about his returning to Georgetown for a few days. "Then I'll come back and help with those Christmas trees."

Soon, he dropped her off at her mom's house. He said he'd be back to take his mom to the Singing Christmas Tree at church on Sunday evening. "I'll probably see you there."

She nodded. "Probably."

She got out, closed the car door, and hurried up the walk. She heard his car leave as she walked through the front door.

Her mom came into the living room as Nancy started to her bedroom to hang up her jacket. "Did you have a good time?"

Nancy laughed. That's the kind of question her mom would ask when she was just a girl, coming in from being with friends. "We caught up on a few things, how the town has changed, the family being here for Christmas. He mainly wanted to express his condolence about Ben's dying."

Her mom didn't say anything. Just stood there. Looking at her. Waiting.

Nancy removed her jacket. "Those cookies smell good. Any left?"

"Plenty. I did take some to Marge. Come on into the kitchen and I'll fill you in."

Her mom turned and headed for the kitchen.

Nancy didn't really want any cookies. Or coffee. But she knew how to go through the pretenses of all being well.

Not that it wasn't. And in the kitchen she would be able to pick up a cup with one hand only and not be afraid it might slip from her grasp.

She walked on into the bedroom and hung up her jacket. At least, he hadn't apologized for rejecting her, for not being able to love her.

Chapter 15

Woody watched Nancy go inside and close the front door of the Walkers' house.

She didn't know where to sit?

As the car moved slowly away, his glance swept over the porch swing. Empty. The last place he and Nancy had sat next to each other. Until today.

He pulled into the driveway and went into his mom's house. She and the nurse knew where to sit. On the couch, watching *The View* on the big screen, critiquing, laughing.

Sophie, beside his mom on the couch, sat up and warned him away with her shrill bark. His mom turned down the volume. "You weren't gone long."

"No." He shrugged. "Wanted to find out when Jim's coming. And let her know I'll help with the Christmas tree."

His mom made a sound. "Jim's coming on Friday, a week before Christmas. His family will stay at the Knight Hotel. So will Don, that's Rebekah's boyfriend. Rebekah will stay at Jean's."

He looked away from his mom's narrowed eyes and the turn of her lips upward. He wanted to say he was a grown man and didn't have to report everything to his mom and did not need her to read anything into a simple little insignificant cup of coffee with a former friend. Instead, he turned his attention to the nurse. "How is Mom?"

The nurse sniffed. "Well enough to let me know she doesn't need me. But she hasn't fired me. Yet. And she lets me eat cookies and watch TV. So I can't complain too much."

Soon it was settled. The nurse would continue to come during the day. His mom had a list of friends who volunteered for the nights. But he would return on Sunday, and maybe the nurse and friends would no longer be needed.

That might depend on how his mom's outing to the Singing Christmas Tree turned out.

Soon, he said his good-byes and headed out toward Georgetown.

Toward what he had called his fulfilled life.

Yes, it had been. But looking over at the empty car seat beside him he wondered what it would have been like if—

No, that would have been an entirely different life.

Driving away from the comfortable town of Silver City and toward the bustling metropolis of DC, he knew he had to let go of the memories. He thought he'd done the right thing by having him and Nancy sit and talk at The Silver Percolator.

They had sat opposite each other.

But she had sat beside him in the car.

Then she went into the Walker house, not sure if that's where she should alight.

They had conversed. Next time, over the holidays, would be easier. The past would be relegated to the past. He would think of it one more time then put it behind him.

Nancy always knew where to sit when they were young. But he kept trying to get her out of her chair and finally accomplished it.

Now as his eyes focused on the increase of traffic as he headed toward the city, his thoughts reverted to that day in the Walker swing, when he'd come to the conclusion that their lives might be swinging in the same direction, but it had proved to be the opposite.

Twenty-three years earlier...

When she returned to him in the swing and sat close enough for their bodies to touch, he took her hand and felt the sensation of its softness. The youthful glow on her face. The eyes shining with emotion, love, anticipation. But he knew that wasn't enough to live on. She'd worked in the summers and saved her money, but she'd lived with her parents who helped out with her tuition.

The temptation was there to tell her to forget college—they'd marry; she could work while he put all his time into studying. To tell her not to seek out any other guys. They could live on love. He could go to class all day, study half the night...but she'd be left to care for an apartment, do the shopping and cooking and cleaning, and work at some kind of job. Not finish her nursing degree. Just live on love...for how long?

How long before that love became drudgery? Before that love was only a few snatches of belonging physically to each other? How long could they live on that? Having her love was the most unexpected, wonderful thing that ever happened to him. He already knew, by experience, that the physical was an enjoyable pleasure that didn't mean a lifelong commitment. He could not chance their love becoming only physical, then fading, then being something that was regretted. When she was seventeen, he hadn't been prepared.

He had to try to look at this like an adult. To support her properly, he needed two more years. Sure, he'd love to take her in his arms, into his life, make her his, and promise her the moon. But that was emotion, and he looked around and saw marriages, and other relationships, that didn't last although they had started with the best of dreams, the best of intentions, and believing everything would work out because they were in love. He'd seen them fail.

He knew two years seemed like a lifetime, particularly to Nancy, being so young. He felt he was always a step ahead of her in maturity. And well he should be, being six years older.

As much as he'd like to take her in his arms and express his undying love, he couldn't. She had two and a half more years of college. To have her make a promise to him while he was in Europe would be unfair. But yes, he could bend his head and touch her lips with his, let his kiss tell her of his love.

But that had been interrupted by Jim and Lauren's arrival.

When he drove away from her, from his hometown, toward his life of obligation, study, personal pleasure, he knew much of it had lost its appeal. His feelings for Nancy had grown deeper, more serious, and he should let her know.

He and Nancy were different. That could mean they complemented each other. She was impulsive, exciting. He was more sensible and focused. She looked at life through rose-colored glasses. He looked at life more realistically. Jim confided in him, even indicated he and Lauren would have had it easier had they waited. He saw their busyness, their frustration, even though they loved each other.

Finally, while in London and so near his goals, he decided he should let Nancy know how he really felt. He carefully crafted the letter, letting his heart speak.

Nancy,
I want you to know this. I've tried to do the right thing,
being older than you. I've tried to do what I thought
our families could approve of, and that's to not inter-
fere with your life and your plans for your own future.
But I do want you to know you've always been spe-

cial to me. You've been a friend, in a much different way than Jim. I've tried to be like a brother to you. But you're more than a sister could be.

My mind, not my selfish heart, wants you to experience life, date guys. I've been that special guy in your life. I've tried to keep seeing you as just a young girl. And I know you are.

But you've wound your way into my heart and into my life, and I can't forget you. I can't make any promises from here. Just know, although I may have seemed vague or uncaring when you said you loved me, I was trying.

Someday, I hope to tell you all that's in my heart.

But for now, just know that I do love you.

You're a wonderful friend. But you're so much more.

Pray for me, think of me, and enjoy life. Have fun in your schooling, in your work. My thesis work requires I remain in Europe during Christmas. I need to get this out of the way so I can get on with my life.

I love you...truly.

Woody

Now, as he neared Georgetown, he thought about that letter. He hadn't made a copy. Looking back on it he thought he probably had not made himself clear. He didn't express his feelings the way Nancy did. Her thoughts were that only love mattered. His were that he could neither fail his dad, nor himself, nor her, and needed to be in a position to support her.

He did know he'd written that his feelings for her went beyond friendship. He signed the letter with more than the usual *Love always*. He had written that he loved her. But he had not proposed. He'd wanted to do it in person.

He'd been too late.

He glanced over at the seat beside him.

Nancy didn't know where to sit.

And the seat beside him was empty.

So he continued on to the life he'd made for himself, to he condo with a view of the Potomac River, the one he told Nancy was a...fulfilled life.

Chapter 16

On Friday evening, Nancy returned to sing at the hospital with the choral group. Afterward, when they had a moment alone in the lounge, Nancy thought about not having had much time to speak personally with Glenda and ask how she was doing. They had been thinking primarily about Mrs. Lawing, just as Woody said he had been.

Now she asked, and Glenda grew teary. "My sister and I are not speaking." Glenda relayed their differences since their mom died, and Glenda, as executor, had done as her mother wished and had her cremated. "Because I'm a nurse, Mom named me medical power of attorney and responsible for having her cremated."

"Helen didn't know?"

"No. She's against cremation, so Mom didn't want to discuss it with her. Now Helen feels we went behind her back and that I talked Mom into it."

Glenda's tears fell. She grabbed a tissue and blotted them away. "I should have told Helen. I should know better, but

I kept thinking I'd find the way and time later." She shook her head. "Three years. We've been together with relatives, but I feel like the distance between us broadens. We aren't speaking...like sisters."

"Please try," Nancy said. "Life is too short to let the past stand in the way of a relationship."

Glenda took a deep breath, batted her moist eyelashes, and resumed her usual demeanor of being in control. "Speak for yourself, Nancy Walker Elrod."

Nancy knew what, or who, she meant.

"Well, for your information, Woody and I *are* talking. We walked Mrs. Lawing's dog together. We had coffee at The Silver Perculator. And we talked."

"Personally?"

"Well, as personal as we could be. I'm trying. It's not easy."

"I know," Glenda said. "You'd think after all these years Helen and I could talk out any problems. But she's hurt. When I asked what she wanted of Mom's things she replied that I'm the one to make such decisions. So, Mom's things are in storage."

"Oh, Glenda. You're right, she's hurting, too. This is the season when thoughts turn more to family. You're all she has. I'll bet she'd love a call from you. I can see this more clearly than you."

Glenda grinned. "I see your and Woody's relationship clearly, too. You didn't spend your life moaning about his not accepting your proposal. You went on to have a wonderful life. A husband and a daughter. You can laugh about that young girl who proposed years ago."

Nancy shook her head.

"I don't mean you have to feel it," Glenda said. "Come on, tell me how funny that is. Make yourself believe it."

"I'll try." Nancy cleared her throat. Then she lifted her face and smiled broadly. "Oh, I was such a silly girl. Going around proposing to men." She moaned and grimaced. "Doesn't work."

"Maybe not," Glenda agreed. "But what you did was done because you loved. What Helen and I did was about a disagreement that led to animosity. She resents me. Woody can't possibly resent you for loving him."

"*Having* loved him," Nancy corrected. "That was years ago. I've had a life since then."

"Exactly," Glenda said. "You have nothing to be embarrassed about. Be honest. You can tell him you feel foolish or whatever, and he will say he knew you'd get over it, and you did because you married and had a good life."

"You're right," Nancy agreed. "Absolutely right."

Nancy felt their gazes weren't as confident as their nodding at each other. "Tell you what," Nancy said. "You give a snow globe to Helen and talk honestly with her, and I'll relax around Woody."

"Sure you will," Glenda said, as if she didn't believe it.

"I can prove it. Come to the Singing Christmas Tree. And bring Helen. I'll save you a seat."

"I'll come," Glenda promised. "Even if Helen doesn't."

Nancy nodded. "Even if she doesn't respond the way you want, you'll know you made that extra effort. And you can move on without regrets."

A light, cold rain fell as Nancy drove home, going through Silver City and seeing the Christmas lights, mostly white on the buildings. Colored lights in store windows, white lights outside, lighted snowflakes and candy canes on telephone poles.

A light rain fell onto the windshield, making a blur of the colorful scene. The wipers sounded a *thump, thump* and then repeated, reminding her of someone shaking her head as if to say shame, shame, no, no.

Even if Helen didn't respond the way Glenda wanted, it was right for Glenda to make the effort.

Although Nancy had felt demolished, hurt, rejected, foolish, and later embarrassed, she had known when Woody did not accept her proposal that she could curl up and die away. Or move on.

Now she knew she'd read too much into that letter of his. She'd seen what she wanted to see instead of his saying they were more than friends. But that didn't mean he wanted to marry her.

Instead of going inside, she drove around the neighborhood for a while, looking at the lights shining from windows. A cold rain outside didn't matter when there was warmth inside. And soon, there would be a tree and decorations in her…in her mom's house.

The scenery began to blur even more, and Nancy wasn't sure if that was because of the moisture outside or inside the car. She drove to her mom's. His car wasn't parked in their driveway. No Christmas lights shone from the Lawing house. Or from the Walkers'. So much…had changed.

That's what she needed to do, and she said so to her mom when she went inside. She decided to get into warm pajamas and curl up on the sofa near the fireplace and bask in its warmth. And in the hot chocolate her mom said she'd make for her.

She would forget about that letter.

But the thoughts persisted even later, long after she snuggled beneath the covers in the same bed that had been hers so many years ago.

She thought of his letter. And her response. It had been right before Christmas break in her sophomore year.

Twenty-three years ago…

"Do you ever miss a single night of writing in that journal?" her roommate Marlene asked, not for the first time.

"Never," Nancy replied. Each night, regardless of how

tired, or how many exams loomed ahead of her, or how late the hour, she sat in bed propped up against a pillow and wrote in the journal. "I pour out my feelings for Woody in this journal, then I can write a decent letter to him without making a fool of myself."

"Love, humbug!" Marlene grinned after she said it then pulled the blanket around her as she turned to face the wall.

Nancy smiled at Marlene's back then at Woody's letter that lay on her journal. She made two kinds of entries in her journal each night. She wrote of her undying love for Woody, her prayers for him, and her hopes for their future. She did not include those in her letters.

Her other entry was a paragraph or two about the events of the day. Then in her weekly letter to him, she would pick and choose from the most interesting or funny happenings that might make him smile or laugh. She always signed the letter, "With all my love, Nancy."

Now, however, she was too full of happiness to tell Marlene about the letter that came today. Her journal entry this night was short. She wrote,

Tonight, in my letter to Woody, I am proposing.

All day, she'd gone through the gamut of reasons why she should, or should not, propose to him. The thought made her shiver with delight. He liked her outgoing personality. She wanted him to know her feelings for him were so much stronger than even when she kissed him when she was seventeen and when he returned the kiss after telling her he would study in Europe for a year.

He had said for her not to wait for him. But that kiss had said so much more. Now his letter confirmed that he loved her. He knew how much she loved him. Now was the time to accentuate that. She wrote the journal entry:

My dearest Woody,

I know you think I'm impulsive, and you're right. But I've thought about this all day, after having thought about it for as long as I can remember. Your last letter meant more than I can say. There is only one possible response I can make.

I have always loved you. I always will.

WILL YOU MARRY ME?

Yours "truly" forever!

Nancy

Nancy had to take a deep breath and exhale it slowly while closing her eyes and leaning her head back into the pillow, lifting her face to the ceiling. A silent prayer played across her brain. The letter was perfect. No need for revision.

Expelling a sigh of relief, she took a piece of her special stationery that bore a picture of a snowman with snowflakes falling around him and along the edges of the paper. That was to remind Woody of their first kiss.

Nancy copied the letter in her best handwriting.

Becoming even bolder, she got out of bed and painted her lips with her best Real Real Red lipstick and made an imprint on the letter. She quickly added a P.S. to the letter: "Sealed with a kiss."

Now that was ingenious of her!

Woody could experience her kiss even from thousands of miles away. She folded the letter so the lipstick could make another pair of lips. The more the better, she decided, smiling.

She slipped the note into the envelope, sealed it, and laid it on top of the Christmas cards she'd addressed to a few friends she wouldn't be seeing during the holiday.

She picked up her journal and entered the date. Beneath that, in bold letters she printed:

TONIGHT, I PROPOSED TO WOODY, THE LOVE OF MY LIFE, FOREVER.

She kissed that page, too, leaving a lighter imprint of her lips than the one on the letter. She grinned. He would have to love that. She almost laughed aloud to think she would love to have an imprint of his lips to kiss.

She zipped her journal and crossed over to the desk opposite her bed and laid the journal in the side desk drawer. She would not write in the journal again until she received Woody's answer. The next entry would be, in bold letters, "HE SAID YES!"

Nancy went to sleep with thoughts of Woody in her life day and night, dreams of their first kiss, their growing love, and their future together.

Early the next morning, while getting ready to take her final exam, Marlene offered to mail Nancy's letters. "I go right by the campus post office on my way to my car. I have to mail mine anyway. I'll be glad to take yours."

Nancy hedged. "I don't know. This is so important."

Marlene glanced at the ceiling then back. "As if I didn't know," she said, looking at the overseas address. "I eat, sleep, and drink that guy daily. Next, I'll be dreaming about him."

Nancy gasped. "You better not!"

Marlene laughed. "I wouldn't know him if he appeared in my dreams. Anyway, you know I have eyes only for George."

"How could I possibly know?" Nancy quipped. "You only talk about George every day, all day long."

Marlene nodded. "I guess we're two of a kind." She tapped the letter. "That's why I know how important this letter is. I'm just making a friendly offer. You and I may never see each other again."

Marlene was a semester ahead of Nancy, and they'd already said their good-byes. Now, Nancy didn't want to be late for her last midterm exam. And she wanted the letter mailed right away.

The quicker Woody received it, the quicker she could begin making her wedding plans. She took a deep breath and reminded herself that Marlene was a dependable person. "Stamps are on the others. But this one goes airmail, you know, and takes extra postage."

Marlene nodded. "I can handle that."

"I know you can," Nancy said. "I'm just...shaky about sending it."

"You know what our Christian Student Group leader says: 'When in doubt, don't do it.'"

Nancy stared at the letter. She wasn't in doubt about her love for Woody. Nor his for her, now. But, would she seem too impulsive? But she thought he liked that about her. He was the sensible one in this relationship. She liked that feeling of being protected and cared for by a responsible man.

Nancy didn't feel comfortable confiding to Marlene that the letter contained a proposal. Marlene wouldn't approve of her taking such a bold step. And besides, this was personal and private. Her proposing was not something to be laughed about or discussed.

"Okay," Nancy said. "Thanks. Write to me sometime."

Marlene nodded. "I'll let you know if I pass the state board exams."

"*When* you pass," Nancy corrected. "Not *if.*"

Marlene nodded. They hugged. Nancy would miss her and wondered what kind of roommate she'd have next.

On second thought, that wouldn't matter. She'd be busy passing finals and planning a wedding to take place ASAP.

"Remember, airmail and extra postage," Nancy said as Marlene walked out the doorway with Nancy's future in her hands.

Chapter 17

If it wasn't so serious, Woody would laugh.

His mom called and said Jean had offered to drive her to the Singing Christmas Tree so he wouldn't need to rush back. He thanked her and said he would drive from DC to the church. That way, he wouldn't need to wonder about where to sit. If he'd gone home first, he'd be expected to drive and take Mrs. Walker and Nancy. Then it would feel ridiculous not to sit with them.

He'd told Nancy that where to sit had never been an issue with him. Now it was. He knew the church women would gather around his mom, and he didn't want to be in the midst of that. Nancy would likely sit beside her mom. He'd feel like a sore thumb sitting beside his mom in the midst of her church women friends.

Then he remembered Nancy said she had sung with a group at the hospital. Maybe she would be in the tree. This was a bad idea. He should have stayed in Georgetown.

However, he pulled into the parking lot that was about one-third filled. Just as he started to get out he saw red backup lights reflected in his car, and he looked in the rearview mirror. In a parking space in back of him, a couple spots down, Nancy was getting out of her car. Her remote sounded, she turned then stopped and stared as he slammed his car door.

Okay, four people who had been friends for years and lived with one house between them drove to the nearby church in three cars. Ah, the incredulity of it.

But maybe there was a good reason. Neither he nor Nancy could pretend not to see each other. She was looking around. For an escape route? Ridiculous. They'd met. They'd talked. They had grown up. They were friends.

"Cold," he said, walking closer to her. Yes, God had been generous to make weather a topic one could always discuss. It's either too hot or too cold to mention those rare times when it's just right.

She nodded.

"Are you singing in the tree?" he asked.

"No. They asked, but they've been practicing for weeks. I haven't been here that long and didn't want to chance being a crow in the midst of canaries."

He laughed. "Never. I've heard you sing."

They walked on to the front door. The pastor in the foyer spoke to them and shook Woody's hand.

"Dr. Lawing," he heard and turned to see Thomas Knight. They moved aside, and after a few words Thomas invited Woody to his home after the service.

Woody responded, "I may need to be home with Mom."

Thomas nodded. "The church has been praying for her."

They talked a little longer. Woody walked to one of the two doorways leading to the sanctuary. A few rows down he saw Nancy. She had removed her coat and draped it over the back of the pew. Was she saving a place for him? Would she want to accompany him to the Knights?

"Woody," his mom's voice said. He turned and faced her

and Jean Walker. "Some of the women are saving us a place. Nancy might already be here. She's hoping her friend will come."

Woody nodded. "I'll sit back here." Seeing people pouring in he hurried to a seat beside an older man on the back row. Was Nancy's friend male or female? At least, instead of not looking at her face in a tree for forty-five minutes or so, he could sit there not looking at the back of her head. She turned her head and glanced toward one doorway then the other. She had a lovely profile. Well, of course. It was the same one she'd had twenty years ago. Her hair was shorter than when she was a college-age girl, but it still fell softly, waving at the ends, to her shoulders. Then he saw her mouth open, and she lifted a hand and motioned.

He took a deep breath. Then exhaled when she stood and three women exchanged words and hugs then sat down.

"You new here?" he heard.

Looking over at the older man he said, "In a way. I grew up here, but I live in DC."

"Welcome," the man said.

Woody had always felt welcome in the house of God. But thanks to Nancy, for the first time in his life, he felt ill at ease about…where to sit.

The pastor stood and welcomed everyone. The choir director walked to the front, his back to the audience; the curtain opened and the huge lighted tree was spectacular. More impressive were the voices that began to sing about the reason for and glory of the season.

The lights were synchronized with the music, various levels lighting different colors at different times, and the huge star on top was a sparkling reminder of the one in the sky two thousand years ago.

Years ago.

Even as his heart and mind felt the wonder of the present, his thoughts drifted to his own life, years ago.

Twenty-three years ago...

She hadn't responded to his letter.

His studies kept Woody busy. His thesis demanded he visit and write about historical places in Europe. He especially enjoyed visiting the castles and cathedrals. Particularly gratifying was news from home. He heard from his mom, with a few words from his dad, at least once a week and sometimes more. He'd missed his family and friends during the Christmas season.

He kept anticipating a letter from Nancy, reflecting her bubbly, enthusiastic personality. And declaring her undying love for him.

It didn't come.

Days then weeks passed, and he received no letter from Nancy.

At first, he told himself she was taking his advice and having fun, enjoying life. The thought caused his heart to lurch within his chest at the thought of her with someone other than him. Had he been remiss in encouraging that? Had he seemed too reticent? Being the mature adult in this situation, what else could he have done?

She had to have her chance to grow up, didn't she? To test her love for him? To make sure?

Sometimes he told himself that he didn't hear from her because he had stressed friendship over love. He'd written about love too lightly. He'd always put his life ahead of hers, and she'd put hers on hold. Or maybe he'd been like a fantasy, the older man, and she now faced reality. Finally, he admitted that Nancy had moved on.

In his letters to his mom and Jim he asked, "How is Nancy?"

Both his mom and Jim wrote that Nancy was well, active as always in school, would work at the hospital during the summer. Jim and Lauren had moved into a house in Silver

City. Jim was then a partner in his dad's accounting firm. He and Lauren were starting their own family.

Woody returned in June for a brief visit after his year in Europe. "Nancy's seeing someone," Jim said that weekend when Woody stopped by to see him, letting him know he had finished his graduate studies and would be going to southern Illinois where he'd been offered a job teaching history at a university. He was now Dr. Woodrow Lawing.

Woody told himself it had to happen. He couldn't think of anything in particular to ask and wasn't sure he wanted to know, but Jim said, "Ben plans to enter seminary after graduation from Towson."

"Seminary," Woody said, nodding. Nancy would consider being a preacher's wife? He supposed he'd been right that her actions toward him had been those of an impulsive teenager who held on to her crush longer than expected. He'd been flattered. No, he'd been floored! Somehow he couldn't picture Nancy in a submissive, behind-the-scenes role like some pastor's wives seemed to fill. No, but she would be innovative, and everyone would know she was her own person. He hoped the fellow would not suppress her outgoing personality.

Jim surprised him by saying, "She's always thought the world of you, Woody."

Woody's glance met Jim's for an instant too long. He forced his gaze to the floor. "That was a long time ago."

Jim surprised him further when he added. "They don't plan to marry for a while. Nancy needs to finish her training, and Ben will be in seminary."

Marry.

Fortunately Lauren, obviously in the family way, came to the doorway and said dinner was ready.

Woody forced his thoughts away.

Later, on the drive home, he felt like the impulsive one. He'd love to go and see Nancy, sweep her off her feet, tell her she belonged with him. But she'd moved on, and away, when she hadn't responded to his confession of love.

She'd done what he'd encouraged her to do for years—to go out with guys—be sure of what she wanted.

He turned a street ahead of where he needed to turn so he would drive by the Walker home. He saw two cars, one in the carport, the other behind it. Those would be Nancy's and her mom's.

He saw the tree where Nancy had given him her sweet kiss on that cold winter's night and warmed his heart forever. He'd passed this way to say to himself it was over. He'd accepted that a long time ago. Then why was he tempted to stop, run inside, and whisk her away?

He drove on past the next house then pulled into his parents' driveway.

He told himself again, like he'd told himself years ago— he'd lost his friend…because of love.

First, she had loved him…when she was too young.

Then, he had loved her…when he was too old.

He flew to Paris for the summer and became reacquainted with Monique. They'd spent time together without either having expectations of a more serious relationship. He thought he would feel free. He'd finished with his studies. He was a doctor. Had a teaching job in Illinois and was assured he would be on staff at Georgetown at the next possible opening. His dad and mom were extremely proud of him.

In the fall he began teaching in Illinois then came home for Christmas. His dad's emphysema was worse, but he'd lived to see his son educated and successful. That made him happy.

Jim invited him to visit during Christmas. Nancy and Mrs. Walker would be there. Jim and Lauren had a newborn baby. Woody longed to see them all. But he knew it would be awkward. Her fiancé might be there. Nancy would be embarrassed. He would feel like a fool—an old one.

He wished Jim a Merry Christmas and told him to tell his

mom and Nancy the same. He would spend part of the holiday with his parents.

On Christmas Eve he and his parents went to the same church they'd always attended. He was greeted by those who'd known him before. He knew a lot of the older people, but the younger ones were either in military service or married and gone. No one asked him out, like they did in the days he and Jim were there. He wouldn't have gone anyway. "I want to walk home," he told his parents after the service.

"You'll freeze," his mom said.

I wish, he thought, but said, "I'll be okay, Mom."

He'd heard the angels sing. He'd praised the newborn king. He needed that cold air to fill his lungs, to freeze his emotions. He neared the Walker house. It was dark. Ice and snow lay on the ground. He stopped at the maple tree and looked in front of the house. No light shone from the windows. No snowman with a carrot nose and coal for eyes and red felt for a mouth that faded against his face as if he'd been kissed and smeared with lipstick.

Woody touched the tree. The cold wind whistled through the bare branches, threatening to shake his own limbs.

He gazed at the streetlight. He'd been mistaken to have thought it emitted a soft glow. He looked away from its harsh glare and walked on.

Houses were lighted with trees in the windows, some bushes outside, and a few with lights across the eaves. But the Walker house was dark. It looked the way Woody felt.

At the door of his parents' house, he stopped and removed one of his gloves. Then he peeled away the thin line of ice that had frozen from his eyes down across his cheeks.

His breath made ghostly wisps in the frigid air.

His lips felt cold.

Chapter 18

Nancy returned home after the Singing Christmas Tree program. She and her mom turned in early, neither wanting TV to spoil the good feeling of the church service. She felt good about Glenda and Helen coming to the church together. They were talking. That was something. She could tell Glenda was being careful in everything she said, instead of displaying her usual openness.

Awkward at first, but a few times putting forth an effort would make all the difference. Just like with her and Woody. They were talking now. Like friends. Not that they'd ever been enemies. It was still rather awkward, but that would vanish. After all, she'd managed to get past her love for him.

With a little time she could get past his rejection. She needed to put the past behind her. She had done that while making a life with Ben. Maybe some of it had been a result of her stubborn determination not to let anything defeat her. She'd always been headstrong, and it came in handy. She would use that now and not let her life be ruled by thoughts of what hadn't been.

The bed was cold. Bereft of human contact. But her thoughts were warm as she touched her wedding rings and thought of Ben.

And what led to Ben.

Twenty-three years ago...

Nancy asked Jim, "Did Woody get my letters?"

"Oh, yes. He appreciated your writing to him. I didn't write as often as I should've, but his mom wrote almost every day, and he got a few from church for a while, too. Seems those people and days are slipping away from us. Everybody's busy with family and jobs now."

Yes, everything had changed. Those good old days were to be cherished. But they were gone. The memories remained— bittersweet.

Nancy had to put a lot of things behind her. Her thoughts, hopes, and dreams had been lost in Woody. Even the finest and best guys at school seemed like immature boys when compared with Woody.

That was, until Ben.

In early spring, she noticed when Ben gave his testimony.

He was a born leader. Maybe because he was a couple of years older than most students. He'd been brought up in a Christian home but got in with a partying crowd. They had more sense than to experiment with drugs, like many of their peers had. But they had no qualms about alcohol.

One night, after a party, Ben was sick. He'd been fighting the flu but went to the party anyway. He couldn't keep the alcohol down, so he was no fun to the others. He'd called his dad who came and picked him up.

That night, three of his closest friends held up a liquor store with their hands in their jacket pockets, pretending to have guns. The proprietor had a real gun. He shot one of the boys and killed him. He held the others captive until the police arrived.

"I have no doubt I would have been with them," Ben said during his testimony. "I was a follower in those days, out to prove that I could be just as bad as the next guy. That changed my life," he said. "I'm still a follower. But now I'm a follower of Jesus Christ. All that partying, alcohol, drugs, gets you nowhere, except dead, or with fried brains, or in prison. It's no fun having a substance take over your life. If you want abundant life, then give it to Jesus."

At the third meeting, Nancy gave her own testimony of having known the Lord all her life but having experienced His presence in a greater way after realizing she was trying to control her own life instead of committing it completely to the Lord. She felt her testimony was not dramatic, but it was real.

Ben talked to her after the meeting. He invited her out for a bite to eat. She planned to drive home for the weekend, but she said yes. He was just as bold about his feelings as he had been about his testimony. "When I saw you last week, Nancy, I knew I could fall in love with you. When I looked at you, everyone else seemed to fade into the background. Now that I've heard you talk, and you're sitting across from me, I want you to know I am in love with you."

Nancy stared at him then down at her hamburger. She looked up again at Ben, such a fine specimen of a man. He was tall, with dark blond hair, cut conservatively and brushed to one side in a self-made wave. His eyes were brown. He was thin. Woody's dark hair waved all over his head in a longer style. Woody's eyes were a dark blue that danced with silvery flecks when the light shone in them. At night, they looked almost black. He was more muscular, and his athletic sport had been football.

Although Woody and Jim both had admitted they had veered from strict Christian discipline, she'd seen their lifestyle of serving the Lord, attending church, and taking part in the activities. They'd been active in youth programs. They'd sung in the choir, as had she. They kept in touch with the church singles when they came home from college. Now, Jim was teaching young boys in Sunday school. Nancy didn't know what Woody was doing. But she knew he was a strong, intelligent, kind, decent, good man.

She'd longed to hear Woody say, "I love you."

He hadn't, except in a way that meant friendship. They didn't even correspond now. She'd ruined that by proposing. How foolish she had been. How immature. But she wasn't immature anymore. And a fine man sat across from her, saying he loved her.

Being loved gave her a warm, comforting feeling.

They ate, drank their milk shakes, then had coffee.

Ben related his intentions of going to seminary and becoming a pastor. "I know this isn't romantic, being done over a cheeseburger, but I wasted my senior year. I dropped out of school. I had become a heavy drinker. I thought I had to have it. My parents saw me through it. I don't want the stuff now. I don't crave it like some alcoholics do. I've tested myself, and I can be around it without wanting it. I want what the Lord offers. I want to spend my life showing others the right way. And, Nancy, I want you by my side."

"You don't even know me," Nancy said.

He put his hand over his heart. "This knows you." He pointed to his head. "And this knows you, too. I don't know how to explain it. Oh, I notice that you're attractive. But so are many other women. It's just…a knowing. Haven't you ever just known you relate to someone?"

She knew exactly what he meant. It's how she had felt about Woody. She had every reason to love Woody. And yet, her love was not because of any of those reasons. There were many men with equally good qualities, but she wasn't in love with them. Yes, love was some unexplainable thing. She couldn't call it an emotion. It was just a knowing.

As she thought about it, she hadn't paid particular attention to Ben during her junior year. But in another sense, she knew him. Because of his transparency, his extroverted way of being open and honest about himself and his ambitions, she knew him better than some people she'd known for years.

Nancy had not considered loving anyone but Woody. But she knew this was serious. Ben wasn't one to play games. His first love was the Lord. But he loved her, too. She hadn't asked or expected to play a part in Ben's life, but she was part of it now.

On the way back to the dorm, she told him about her love for Woody. She explained it as a childhood crush that had developed into love. She still loved him but didn't know how to define or relate it on any scale from one to ten. She loved him, but they apparently weren't meant to be together.

Ben remained silent until after he parked his car near hers. He switched off the engine then turned and faced her. The night was clear, and the moonlight lighted his brown eyes that looked at her with love that held no reservation.

"Since I feel so strongly about this," he said, "will you give me a chance to love you?"

A wonderful man wasn't begging her to love him. He was asking for a chance to love her. How unique. Of course he would want her love in return, but this showed an incredible unselfishness. He just wanted…a chance.

"There are finals coming up," she said. "Then I'll be working at the hospital all summer."

"The same goes for me," he said. "But can we see each other occasionally?"

Nancy nodded.

Ben raised his hand to her chin and leaned toward her. Nancy met him halfway. They kissed. His lips were warm and firm. The kiss was sweet then full of desire, and they broke away.

"I love you," he said with meaning.

Nancy nodded again. "Thank you."

She turned and got out of the car. He waited until she got into her car then followed her to the main road and turned in the direction of his dorm. Nancy drove home.

She parked in the driveway behind her mom's car. Walking along the concrete walk in front of the porch, she looked over at the big maple tree. Tears filled her eyes.

"Honey, what's wrong?" her mom said when she entered the living room.

Nancy couldn't hold back the sobs any longer. She'd already told her mom about Ben, the outstanding man who'd given his testimony in front of the student body then became leader of the CSG.

"Ben loves me," she said.

Her mom laid down her magazine and held out her arms to Nancy, who rushed over, sat on the floor, and put her head on her mom's knees. Her mother stroked her hair. "It's good to be loved," she said.

Nancy nodded against her mom's knees as she cried.

A chance, he'd asked.

Why wouldn't she love Ben?

She wondered if Ben would pursue her. She should have known better. He'd made himself clear about his feelings and his intentions. The next move would be hers.

Two weeks later, after several from the CSG had gone to a nursing home to sing and Ben to give a brief talk, she asked if he would take her back to her car last. He nodded.

That night when he reached for her, she yielded to his embrace and his kiss.

Nancy didn't know if he thought that was her declaration of love or if she was just giving him a chance. He didn't ask, and she didn't say. They began to see each other at every rare opportunity.

She stopped comparing Woody and Ben. There was no comparison. Nancy was filling her life with Ben. She felt special. She was loved.

The night she told Ben she loved him, he cried.

And now, two years after Ben's death, Nancy thought of their love for each other. She held a pillow close and felt the wetness seep around her closed eyes.

Chapter 19

Whether she was beginning to accept him or had jumped up on top of the bed and yapped in his face to warn him to get out of her house, Woody pushed Sophie off the bed and pulled the covers over his head.

That surprised him.

But it did not surprise him a short while later when he sat at the breakfast table and his mom said, "Jean thought instead of her going with you to pick out our trees, Nancy might go with you."

"You don't feel like going?"

"I know I'm much better," she said, "but last night I felt the pressure or whatever it is, a little more than I have been." She touched her chest on the right side to indicate the spot. "And I was very tired. I'm all right now, but I'd rather save my energy to decorate the tree instead of picking it out."

He agreed it was best his mom didn't venture out into the damp, cold day and search for a Christmas tree. But he also knew what she and Jean Walker would be thinking. After all, he was a bachelor and Nancy a widow. Perfect match, eh?

Little did they know he was trying to reaccept what he'd accepted years ago. He thought he was over having lost out by trying to be sensible, practical, and realistic.

The more he and Nancy related, the more comfortable and accepting he would feel. "She's helping her mom get ready for Christmas with their family. So I'm not going to ask her to go with me to pick out a tree."

"Jean will," his mom said.

So it was settled. He called the lot and asked if they delivered. They did, so after his mom told him Jean said Nancy would go, he drove up to the Walker house and Nancy came out, wearing jeans, tennis shoes, and a jacket with a hood.

She hopped in. "Ah, warm in here," she said. "It's blustery out there."

He studied her for a long moment. Watched her avoid his gaze, peer out beyond the windshield. She didn't look at him, the way she hadn't looked at him a long time ago.

She pushed back her hood and her hair tumbled around her face, even more beautiful than when she was younger. A hint of fragrance suffused the air. He remembered her best in the cold, in the snow, a scent of female and fragrance. He sensed it now.

He'd had enough. He'd never been the impulsive type. Always the thinker.

He was tired of it. Tired of being careful. "Nancy." He heard the urgency in that one word. A world, a world he had missed, was in that name. Why deny it? "Are you in a hurry?"

Her face turned toward him. For an instant he thought he could get lost in the depth of her dark eyes. As if she, too, were caught up in the small world of only the two of them in the dark interior, the rest of the world shut out. She gazed at him. Not like in ages past. But like, maybe, seeing someone she didn't know.

Did she want to?

Finally, she spoke softly. "I have nowhere in particular to go."

Did that mean she was indifferent?

At least, she was not adverse to going somewhere when the other option was nowhere.

He reached over and picked at the edge of her jacket hood. Her head moved slightly, and he felt a few soft hairs against his fingers, and he moved them away and thought he should let her know he wasn't trying to be familiar, but they were—

"We're old friends, Nancy—"

"Ah!" She gave his hand a quick hit. "Speak for yourself. You'd think a university professor would know better than—"

"I do. Believe me. I didn't mean—"

She laughed. "We know our ages, Woody."

"Yes, we do." For the first time. In such a long time. He saw a little spark of the—not older, but former Nancy in her eyes. The playfulness. He laughed. Why? Because he...felt good. "How long since you've been to DC?"

Her hesitation lasted only the length of a breath. "A while."

"Want to see where I live? How I live?"

Her chin lifted, but the spark remained. "I would love to see your...fulfilled life."

She remembered what he'd said. He remembered, too. And he had believed it. And so, when he revved the motor and struck out of there, only for an instant, playfully, she gave him a sidelong look, fastened her seat belt, and headed with him toward the big city.

On the way to his Georgetown home, he began to tell her about his life of teaching and the places he took his students, not just abroad but more importantly right there in the nation's capital. "But you lived here," he said.

She looked over at him. "I was young then and took DC for granted. And of course I've known of the historic places. But I haven't even visited them all. When we visited here, we took Rebekah to the Smithsonian and of course walked by the White House. We never went inside to tour it."

So he gave her a few history lessons; much she would know, of course, but he was accustomed to bringing out the dates, the reason for certain buildings, their importance to the nation and to the world.

"Do you know," he said, feeling the sadness of it, "some of my students didn't even know about the Holocaust until they came to my class. Many who have lived around DC all their lives had never visited the World War II Memorial."

"I haven't," she said. "I'm beginning to see that students, including my Rebekah, could really have benefited from knowing more about our country and our nation's capital."

He nodded. "Like you mentioned, we take so much for granted instead of thinking about the sacrifices that have been made for us." He decided to venture further, thinking of Nancy's daughter who had lost her dad not too long ago. "I met Rebekah, you know. Several times at Jim's. And through the years I've seen her. In passing. At your mom's."

"I know," she said. "She likes you. She says you know more about our nation's capital than Jim and me put together."

He laughed. "I teach it. So I have it memorized."

"She's impressed."

"When Rebekah and Don come, I'd be glad to show them around DC."

He felt the pause before she softly said, "Thank you." He wondered if she were wishing Rebekah's dad were there to visit important places with his daughter. But of course she would be. He'd had many students who were without their parents for numerous reasons, and he'd been told many times he was like a dad. *Like* a dad wasn't *being* a dad though.

"Oh, how lovely," she said when he turned into the historic neighborhood lined with trees.

"The residents of this area are very fortunate. We have the

best of history and upscale facilities. There's opportunity for outdoor activity—walking, jogging, biking, boating."

"Looks and sounds amazing." She looked out the windows, from one side to the other.

He thought she was equally impressed with his luxury condo. He'd become accustomed to the full-service residence, twenty-four-hour concierge service, a door attendant, and the on-site manager.

Driving into one of his two private parking spaces in the underground garage, he mentioned the rooftop pool.

"Oh, so that's how you have kept in shape."

He pretended surprise. "You think I'm shapely, huh?"

She laughed. "Not exactly that."

He laughed with her. "I will admit staying fit becomes increasingly more difficult. But, the gym helps, too."

"I understand," she said. "Fortunately, we did quite a bit of hiking in the mountains of North Carolina. The views are fantastic."

They got out of the car. "I haven't been to your mountains," he said, "but one of my greatest pleasures is the view from my unit."

Inside in the living room, Nancy commented favorably on the decor.

He saw it as he thought it would look in her eyes. Pristine, off-white walls; ivory white, comfortable plush couch, love seat, and chairs suitable for a man, inviting to guests. A much cleaner look than a home with children and animals. The colorful wool rug beneath the glass-top coffee table was from, of course, Europe.

"Are those originals?" She glanced around at the paintings on the walls. "None," he said, not bothering to say they were expensive reproductions. "Except the one in my study, over the fireplace." He motioned, and she followed him into the next room. Seeing her smile he thought that was the kind of room she liked most. Cozy, with an afghan thrown carelessly across the arm of the recliner near the fireplace. Bookshelves covered two walls, and a desk sat in front of one. A couch was along one wall. But she knew. "This is your favorite place."

He nodded and gestured at the painting above the mantel. "That's a Thomas Knight original."

The wistfulness in her eyes was unmistakable before her gaze left him and focused on the painting of his mom and dad. He felt sure she was thinking the same as he. Her dad had died unexpectedly.

Her brother, Jim, had told him their dad and mom had gone to a nearby town to celebrate their wedding anniversary. James had eaten steak, rare the way he liked it, and later that evening had to be taken to the hospital with stomach pains. He died of food poisoning.

Woody's dad lived five years longer, a blessing they hadn't expected. Woody had come to both funerals. At each, Nancy's husband had been with her, to comfort her.

Her gaze fell to the gas fireplace. "We had a wood-burning one in North Carolina. This is cleaner." She walked over to the window and stood looking at the Potomac River. He came up beside her. She turned and asked softly, "Do you decorate for Christmas?"

"If Mom or someone is coming here for the holidays, I'll put up an artificial tree."

Her face turned again to the window. He wondered if his luxury condo seemed artificial to her. He gestured to the boats on the river. "At night there's a river adorned with lighted boats right outside my window. And not too far away there's the national Christmas tree on the lawn of the house that belongs to us all."

She glanced at him. "Good speech."

Liking the playfulness, he said, "I tried. But, um, you think a real tree belongs in here?"

She turned and pointed to the fireplace. "Right there. You

have the recliner at one side. The other side could use a tree." She smiled. "Even an artificial one would do."

He was now aware that side did look a little empty. But this was an ultra-modern bachelor pad. "That *is* where I put the artificial one."

He wondered what was behind her thoughtful expression. Then she said, "Do you have ornaments from other countries?"

For an instant he stiffened, afraid she might ask if he still had a few mementos she'd given him ages ago. He didn't know. He'd kept things in a drawer when he lived at home. But after she was married, he would not consider putting a reminder of her in a drawer or on the tree. "Actually, many of my ornaments are from other countries, and some depict historic places in DC."

"Conversation pieces," she said. "I've wondered what men do since it's women who make scrapbooks."

"I have a few of those," he countered. "But, getting back to decorations, I have a beautiful carved-wood crèche that I always set out on the mantel."

He wondered if she might ask to see his souvenirs. She looked over at him and said, "You do have a rich, fulfilled life, don't you?"

He stepped back. "Let's go into the living room." When they did, he gestured to one of the white chairs. He thought it best she not sit in his recliner, or in his study. Already she invaded his mind and memories so much. "Come and sit. Here," he said, wanting her in a certain chair.

He sat on the couch opposite her and took a deep breath. Nothing to lose. He'd already lost her. He would try to gain a comfortable camaraderie. Already they were talking personally. "I do have a fulfilled life, Nancy."

"But you never married."

He looked down at his European rug for a moment, not feeling snug as a bug, however. "I have known some intriguing, charming women. But when it came to considering a life-time with them, I couldn't commit to that. None occupied my heart and mind so completely."

He was glad she wasn't looking at him then, but at the rug, or the coffee table on which sat a vase from Paris holding artificial green leaves.

"There came a time," he said, "when I had to give up a personal life of a particular kind. Guilt and maturity finally caught up with me."

Her questioning gaze met his then.

"After I began teaching at Georgetown I became close with another teacher. I knew this particular woman wanted marriage. I didn't. I knew she thought I'd give in. And one day, I said offhandedly to God, 'God, You don't expect me to be a saint all my life, do You?' I wasn't really talking to Him. But apparently He was listening. The next day the pastor paid a visit. He asked me to teach a class of college students. I said I'd think about. He said to pray about it. I didn't pray about it. What would I pray? 'Lord, let me know if I should lead a celibate life and teach those young people, or if I should do what I want when I want, after all I'm only human.'"

He grimaced.

Nancy grinned. "So," she said, "how long have you been teaching the class?"

He laughed. "Several years. Not easy but very fulfilling." He found that by telling the students, male and female, about the decisions he made, those choices made an impression.

He, at that moment, wanted Nancy to know that he often wondered if he'd made the wrong choice back in his twenties. Yes…he told his class; he would tell Nancy.

"I'm able to say things in the Sunday school class that I don't say in the university classroom. You see, Nancy, there's a lot to the saying that hindsight is twenty-twenty. I know my reasons for my choices. I couldn't fail my dad. And I wanted to be successful. I did not think I should ask you to wait for

me indefinitely, although I wanted you to. I did not think
marriage was the answer to our—"

He paused. He couldn't call it a relationship. "Our situation. Thinking back, my own selfishness was probably part
of it, too. If I'd made a commitment to you, I'd have to give
up my girlfriends. After all, I told myself, I was a grown man
still in his twenties."

She had clasped her hands on her lap. She might very well
be thanking God she'd found Ben, a man with a great commitment to the Lord, instead of a selfish, self-serving one.
One who hadn't trusted his own heart and mind.

She didn't ask any questions, but he wanted to say the
most important thing. "Back then, I wanted it all. My personal life with no strings attached, a wonderful young girl
waiting back home; although I had enough sense to tell her
not to, I thought she always would be there. Guilt and maturity finally caught up with me."

She was quiet, but a little smile touched her lips, so he continued. "I miss having an intimate life with women. But I've
discovered that what you think, what you do, what you aspire
to, you become. I'm far from perfect, but my top priority is to
be the man God wants me to be and an example for those young
people. So, yes, my life has empty spots, but it's a fulfilled life."

Perhaps he chose wrongly in those early years, responded
wrongly. But God still saw fit to use him. One should be
thankful for lessons learned from failures and successes.

"At the university I'm recognized, officially acclaimed as
being a noteworthy professor of history." He smiled at her,
certainly didn't want her to think he was bragging. "And that's
important. But God and I know my real accomplishment is
not in relating history but in relating His story." He paused.
"And, the Sunday school class is my accountability. My actions abroad and in the university are watched."

"I understand that," she said. "That's how it was as a
preacher's wife. I aspired to being the best wife I could be,

a support and helpmate to Ben. The kind of wife a preacher needed. How good I was, I can't judge, but it was my best."

He stood and held out his hands. After his confessions, she would know he wanted them to be friends. He hoped she knew he forgave her for rejecting him.

She placed her hand in his and stood. He felt the rings on her finger and let go. "Now, why don't I show you what a Potomac River bachelor's sandwich is like. Then we'll go and pick out those Christmas trees."

She agreed.

"There's this corner place called The Gatsby Arrow," he said, as he drove into Georgetown, "that has a French diner feel to it."

She agreed to that, too.

After they were inside and served their sliced roast beef, hot with lettuce and tomato on a French baguette, she moaned with pleasure at the first bite. "This baguette might be the closest I'll ever get to France."

"Perhaps not," he said. "You can come and go as you please, can't you?"

She combined a hint of a smile with the lift of an eyebrow and a shoulder. Then she nodded at the sandwich in her hand and said, "This is good."

If instead, she had said, "With whom?" he would have told her.

Chapter 20

On the way to the Christmas tree lot in Silver City, Nancy settled into the close confines of the black sports car's interior. This man was not the Woody she had known. She was getting to know the man Woody had become. He'd said that what you aspire to, you become.

He had crossed over the hurdle of studies, schooling, teaching experience, holding on to self, and had settled into being a fine man, fulfilling a wonderful purpose, having meaning in his life. He was settled, his life secure, and he traveled throughout Europe. He understood the importance of the nation's capital city and wanted to instill patriotism and pride in his students.

This was Dr. Woodrow Lawing, and she was beginning to know and like him.

They picked out the Christmas trees, and the lot attendant said they'd be delivered that afternoon.

When Woody pulled up to the front of her mom's house, Nancy put her hand on the door handle, but he said, "Nancy."

She looked over at him. This man she had known, didn't know, was getting to know.

"Thank you for today. And for listening to me. It seemed to be all about me. I would like to hear about you. Could we do that some evening? Have dinner together?"

She didn't want to sound too eager. "After you get those Christmas trees set up, our moms will want to decorate. But I'm free…" She thought of saying *forever* then thought no, she was free until the family came in; so she said, "Oh, Mom goes to a Bible study at church on Tuesday evening." She waved a questioning hand.

"Sounds like a plan," he said. "The Knight Hotel suit you?"

"I'd like that. We went there when we visited a few years ago. Then it was closed for several years. And after what you told me about Thomas Knight, that sounds like it could be an interesting evening."

She wondered for a moment at the expression that marred his handsome face. "Oh," she gasped and then laughed. "I don't mean to say that it wouldn't be interesting if the place wasn't."

His laugh was low and comfortable. Then he grew serious again. "I'm sure hearing about your life will be interesting."

"Thank you," she said, turning to open the door.

"Tell your mom I'll come to set up the tree."

"Thanks again," she said.

When she went inside, her mom said, "Did you find the right trees all right?"

"Wasn't too difficult. They'll deliver this afternoon."

"You hungry?"

"We had lunch."

"Mmm."

"It was nice," she said. "Getting reacquainted. Well, we never were really acquainted. I mean he was Jim's friend. Just because we were neighbors didn't make us know each

other. And he was older. Is older. So, I guess we were jus
getting acquainted."

"I see," her mom said and went over to brush at the back
of the couch as if something were on it. "After the trees are
up, I'm going down to help Marge with decorations."

"I want to call Rebekah," Nancy said. "And I have some
laundry to do. I'll cook dinner tonight. Probably need to go
to the supermarket."

"I've started a list."

Nancy followed her mom into the kitchen. By the time
she was ready to shop, the trees had arrived and theirs was
put in the carport.

"I'll go on down," her mom said. "Marge and I want to
snap pictures of the ornaments and make a little booklet of
the memorable ones for our children and grandchildren."

"That's a great idea, Mom. I might do something like that
for Rebekah. Just like you, we have ornaments represent-
ing all kinds of events, even my and Ben's first Christmas
together."

"You want to come?"

She shook her head. "I think the two of you will have a
better time reminiscing without me," Nancy said. "After supper we can get your decorations out and be ready for you and
Marge to start here in the morning."

"It's beginning to feel like Christmas." Her mom looked
happy. "Oh, I'll call Marge and see if she needs anything
from the store since you're going."

"And since I'm going to cook, and Woody's putting up
trees, why don't I cook enough for them, too."

Her mom liked the idea. "Oh, invite them here?"

Nancy said no, they shouldn't invite them, but someone
could take the food down.

When Nancy returned from the supermarket, Woody had
put the tree in its stand and set it beside the fireplace. Her

mom said Woody would pick up the supper when it was ready, just give him a call.

She liked cooking up a southern-fried chicken dinner for four instead of what she often did, which was to wonder what to fix for just herself. She also thought about the day with Woody. She'd known he had girlfriends. After all, he was her brother's friend. And he was twenty-three when she first declared her love for him.

He and Jim had special girls when they were young. But she'd seen him with a woman only once.

Twenty-two years ago...

She and Ben were engaged. Nancy never asked about Woody, afraid her voice might give away the emotions she felt when she thought of him and how she had loved him and had built up in her mind that he loved her, too. Every once in a while, her mom or Jim would make a remark about what Woody was doing. He kept in touch with Jim.

"Nancy," her mom said one evening in late November, after Thanksgiving, as they sat in front of the fireplace, each reading a novel. "Marge says Woody is coming home for Christmas."

That skip of her heartbeat was only from memories of her past, she told herself. "Really." She stared at the novel she laid on her lap. "What's he doing now?"

"Jim said he's still teaching history at a university in Illinois."

"That far away?" That was in another state. However, it wasn't as far as Europe.

As soon as she said it, Nancy reminded herself that she was no longer a teenager in love with an older man who lived two houses away. They both had moved on. Woody had moved to another state. After she married Ben, she would go to Ken-

tucky while he continued in seminary, then they'd go where
the Lord led.

She absently fingered the engagement ring Ben had given
her during the summer. She and Ben had picked it out when
he'd come home during the summer.

Woody was coming home for Christmas.

So was…Ben.

The two of them planned to set a wedding date during
the holiday.

Ben drove in from Kentucky on Christmas Eve. Jim and
Lauren and their toddler came home for Christmas. They,
too, arrived on Christmas Eve. They all attended the candlelight service at church.

Nancy was with Ben and wondered how she would feel if
Woody was at church with a woman. Then she knew. They
sat near the back, and Nancy got a good look standing at the
doorway then again as she walked down the aisle. She was
a blond. Dark blond. Ash, she supposed. Pulled back, looking sophisticated, with a long strand falling along her…sort
of attractive face. Older than Nancy. Well, so was Woody.

She looked rather perfect, in face and figure. She looked
up at Woody the way Nancy envisioned having looked at him
when she was just a girl in love with him.

When Nancy passed their row, Woody smiled at the ash-
blond then looked ahead at the singing choir, and that reminded Nancy of how reserved he had been with her. He was
being reserved now, because he was in church, and behaved
maturely. What about when he and the woman were alone?

No! She mustn't think about that. She needed to think
about when she and Ben were alone. When her family took
their seat, she reached over and laid her hand on Ben's. He
held her hand in his warm, firm grip. She looked at him. He
looked at her like the ash-blond had looked at Woody.

I am loved, Nancy thought then forced her attention to
the choir, and the words, and the meaning of this night when

the angels sang, *"Glory to God in the highest, and on earth peace, good will toward men."*

After the service, Jim and her mom were introducing Ben to members. When Nancy heard that familiar voice say, "Good to meet you," she looked around, and her gaze rested on Woody. Their gazes met and held. Somehow she managed to hold out her hand when he introduced Dr. Frances Ily.

Nancy felt a numbness as she shook Frances's hand and looked at the woman's face and her light blue eyes. She was even prettier up close. Not a hair was out of place, and her lips were coral.

Woody must think Nancy a complete dud. No, he wasn't the kind of person to think derogatory things. He simply wouldn't be impressed with her. Likely, she still looked like a girl compared to Dr. Frances. But then, there was no competition. After she had proposed to Woody, she hadn't received a personal letter again. That silence spoke loudly.

Jim suggested they walk the few blocks home, like they used to. He seemed to want to renew the old days. He had his memories. Nancy wanted to run away from hers. But Lauren thought that was a great idea, and Dr. Frances said it sounded lovely.

Nancy looked at Ben, whose expression meant it was up to her. Why would she not want to? "Sure," she said.

Nancy's mom said, "Stephen can ride home with me." She looked at Woody and his parents. "Join us for hot chocolate?"

Nancy felt as uncomfortable as Woody looked. He didn't wait for his parents to respond but said, "We plan to open presents tonight. But thanks."

The night glowed bright with an almost-full moon and many stars. No snow had fallen, nor was it in the forecast. The slight breeze was brisk, a great night for walking a few blocks.

She was glad Woody didn't want to come inside. He'd always been like a part of her family in so many ways. But he'd moved on...as had she.

On the walk home, it was different than in the old days. Instead of her leading the conversation and teasing Woody, she stayed mostly silent, and Jim asked the questions, mainly to Frances. He knew about everyone else. Frances was teaching English in Illinois. Woody brought her all the way from Illinois. It must be serious.

Nancy was wearing an engagement ring. She had peeked at Frances's left hand but saw no ring. Maybe tonight Woody would ask Frances to marry him. The thought struck her like a blast of cold winter wind. Only, she told herself, because she'd lost her friend. Marriage was so final.

Nancy felt loved with Ben walking close to her, holding her gloved hand. His presence made her feel secure. Jim and Lauren didn't hold hands, but they were married. Woody and Frances didn't, but maybe they were too mature, or too doctorish. She was not. She felt safe with her hand in Ben's.

"Sure you won't come in?" Jim said when they reached their home.

"No," Woody answered. "We have to go on."

The earlier thought returned: maybe Woody would give Frances an engagement ring tonight. Could he do such a thing at Christmastime, in the winter, where he could see the maple tree in her yard? Could he have forgotten that kiss? And the one before he went to Europe? Could he forget her so easily?

His letter to her from Europe, the one that prompted her to propose, had reaffirmed that he cared for her. But even the friendship they had shared had slipped away, ticked away with every movement of the hands on a clock, sunk each evening with the sun into the horizon. Their friendship could be only a memory. But what purpose did such a memory serve?

He had always been more than a friend in her heart. That had to change. He had a girlfriend…no, a woman friend… no, a doctor friend. And Nancy was engaged to be married.

She could not envision her and Ben, Woody and Frances being friends. Once she'd gone beyond *friend* there was no turning back. She mustn't go backward to what couldn't be. She must go forward to what lay ahead.

Everyone said the expected amenities. She felt that Woody didn't even want to speak to her. He must be as uncomfortable as she; however, he hadn't been the one to make the advances. That had been her own impulsiveness. Jim and Lauren went on up the walk.

Woody stopped and turned to Nancy and Ben. He looked at Ben. "Take good care of my friend." Then he shifted his gaze to Nancy. "Be happy," he said low.

Nancy knew his expressions. He looked like something inside him was tearing him apart. Likely, he feared she would be embarrassed over her impulsiveness in the past.

"I will," was all she could say. She couldn't manage to be as generous as he and say, "You be happy, too." For an instant she wanted him to be miserable. Deep inside, of course, she *did* want him to have a good life.

The night was silent, as if the world held its breath. Nancy neither heard nor saw anyone, in that moment, except Woody.

He almost smiled, but it didn't reach his eyes. "Merry Christmas," he said.

Ben responded, "Merry Christmas."

When Woody turned away, Nancy's instinct was to run after him, hold him tight, and tell him she would always love him, would always remember him, would always hold him in her heart.

But fortunately she'd learned to control her impulsiveness. It had only made a fool of her. When Woody's arm slid around Frances's waist and the ash-blond looked up at him, Nancy quickly looked at Ben. Maybe he would think the cold air stung her eyes and made her blink that way. She just needed to be loved.

Ben put his arm around her shoulders. She didn't feel she had the voice to explain Woody more than she had the first time she and Ben went out together. Ben didn't ask. He was there, with his comforting arm, his expression of undivided love for her. He leaned close and said, "I love you with all my heart, Nancy."

Her heart was too full of memories and the maple tree to dishonor Ben by saying she loved him at that moment. She would tell him later. She did love him. Not in that youthful, impulsive way. But in the mature, serious way of people who know love is not just a feeling but a decision of commitment to build a life together.

She and Ben had talked about discussing wedding plans during this Christmas season. "Summertime," she would say, "when the sun is shining and it's warm."

She couldn't bear to think of a wedding in winter, with snow on the ground. That would bring too many memories that needed to stay frozen in the past.

Chapter 21

"That aroma is supper?" Woody said when he walked into the kitchen to pick up the food Nancy had wrapped up and set into a box.

"Southern cooking."

"Not grits?"

"Sure. And fried okra."

He grimaced.

Nancy laughed. "Kidding. But if you haven't tried it, don't knock it."

"Point taken." He inhaled heavily. "Anything that smells like this has to be good."

Later, while she and her mom were cleaning up the kitchen, Marge called to thank them. She said Woody told her to give his compliments to the chef and said southern-fried chicken competed well with the local seafood.

Nancy liked the compliments. And having cooked for several people. Many times she wasn't sure what to have for dinner anymore. Cooking for one wasn't as easy or as enjoyable as sharing food with someone else. Even if some of them were…two houses away.

As soon as the kitchen was cleaned and they walked into the living room, Nancy breathed in the aroma of cedar. Her mom touched a limb of the full-branched tree. "It's a pretty one. Let's bring up the boxes of decorations. Marge will come after breakfast in the morning so we can get an early start."

"You finished with hers?"

"Oh no, but the lights are on and many of the ornaments. It takes more time since we're photographing and writing. We could go ahead and put the lights on ours."

Seeing how anxious her mom was, Nancy agreed. She was getting into the Christmas spirit herself.

Several boxes were marked as decorations. They hauled boxes up and set them in the living room. "Now, if I can just find the lights," her mom said.

Nancy opened a box. "Mom, these are not decorations." Inside were books and papers. Then she began to recognize them. "These are from my old college days."

Her mom waved a hand. "I've done that same thing and brought those boxes up. Some of your things and some of Jim's are still down there. You should look through them and see if there's anything you want."

"I will. They can probably be thrown away or given away."

Nancy lugged a couple boxes into her bedroom. She returned to the living room where her mom had found the lights. She took out the big star that always topped the tree.

Her mom became reminiscent. "I haven't even put all the ornaments on in the past years. And had an artificial tree. These bring back memories." She couldn't resist holding up one ornament then another as they talked about the meanings of some and remembering when Nancy's dad was with them.

"Woody gave us this little sled. That boy was almost as much of the family as Jim. I used to think—"

Nancy glanced at her mom. Her mom laid the ornament

on the coffee table and took out another. She didn't finish her thought. Nancy didn't ask. It didn't really matter what her mom used to think.

Then she said, "I used to wonder if you'd ever get over the crush you had on that boy."

"I never said anything like that."

Her mom gave her the look she'd used when Nancy was just a little girl and said she hadn't sneaked a cookie while crumbs dotted on her face, or she wasn't the one who colored the wall while she still held the crayon.

"Nancy. Moms know a few things." She gave her a knowing look. "You have a daughter."

Nancy hadn't given her mom enough credit. Nancy thought of her own daughter. Just a glance could tell her if Rebekah was in love, serious, sad, embarrassed, angry. Yes, moms knew a lot about their daughters.

"Well, as you know, I did get over the crush. I married, remember? Ben and I had a wonderful marriage."

Her mom smiled. "I know, dear. I had that with your dad. But, did I ever tell you about the boy I loved in the first grade? And the one in high school? And the doctor I met when I volunteered at the hospital?"

"Mom, you were married when you volunteered at the hospital, weren't you?"

She put her hand on her chest. "Oh my, yes. Forget I said that. Let's go back to Tommy in the first grade."

They both burst into laughter. Nancy figured she and her mom might be able to live together and be friends after all. But only one of them seemed keen about that idea. She liked these glimpses of her mom as a human being and not just a mom.

That brought to mind her last conversation that afternoon with Rebekah, who said Don wanted them to pick out an engagement ring during Christmas.

Nancy had already given much thought to her rings. She would not take them off at the Asheville church because she didn't want to cause any room for disagreement or gossip. But she had told Rebekah a long time ago the rings would someday be hers. She had expected it to be after her death, not after Ben's.

But on the phone she'd said, "Rebekah, my wedding rings are yours at any time. If you want the engagement ring now, that's fine. I understand if you don't. Just let me know."

Rebekah had loved the idea, but she needed to discuss it with Don. Nancy understood he might feel it more personal to buy a ring that Rebekah picked out and he paid for.

But…she might give the wrong impression if she removed the rings, now at the Christmas season, when she'd come home and was becoming friends with the mature Woody.

"Oh," she said, her attention being drawn to her mom who plugged in the string of colored lights, which then glowed against the floor. "I'll get the stool while you test the others, and we'll get this tree ready. Amazing what colored lights can do for the Christmas season."

"Isn't it!" her mom said. "Oh, Nancy. I know we've had wonderful holidays together. But with the circumstances as they are, I'm so glad you're home this Christmas."

"I am too, Mom." She felt at home. She would probably stay until after the New Year. And then? Well, she never was good at guessing what the future had in store. She had learned to be content. Mostly. Right now she felt…rather content.

Later, after the lights were aglow on the tree, she and her mom watched TV and ate popcorn. It had been a good day. A good evening.

After going to bed, however, she wondered if she could remain content when everyone returned to their lives after the holiday that seemed to be working up toward a wonderful one. What about when Jim and his family left? When Rebekah and Don returned to their busy lives and their plans with each other? What about… ?

No.

She had friends in North Carolina. She could work again at a hospital or take another private nursing job, or even volunteer at a hospital. She could have a…fulfilled life. Or she could find a house in or near Silver City. There were many possibilities.

But for now, she should accept the days as they were. Today had ended, so she would think about tomorrow. Woody said he wanted to know about her.

What did she learn most about him? His faith. So she would tell him the most important part of her story—when she'd made a mature commitment. That's the important thing, not where she had lived or that she had a husband and child. Of course they were of utmost importance to her. But they were family, blessings common to mankind. She had weaknesses, failures, successes, regrets, hopes, like all humans. He didn't need to know her hobbies, her trips, the places where she'd lived. The important thing was her faith.

As he had told of his, that outshone his education, his knowledge, his lovely home, the view of the Potomac River, his travels. No, it was his faith. Today, she'd met a man of faith.

It tended to make her more aware, bring a sense of contentment, peace, acceptance. Ben showed her God's acceptance, not rejection. She remembered when she felt her commitment to God and her family had reached a deeper, new level.

When Rebekah was born, Nancy felt she had fulfilled her role of being a woman. Never had she felt such an incredible sense of responsibility, mingled with joy. God and Ben had given her a most precious gift.

"I wasn't called to be a preacher," she said early in their marriage after Ben had gently instructed her not to tell Flora Brown to mind her own business when the woman had said she shouldn't let her daughter run through the sanctuary pretending to be an airplane because that was sacrilegious.

Nancy had replied that it's more sacrilegious to think that a child even knew the meaning of that word. Rebekah was God's wonderful creation, having fun in the house of God, and wasn't hurting anything. Besides, the sanctuary was wood and carpet and padded pews, not religious objects. King David had danced naked before the Lord. A child could at least pretend to be an airplane.

But Nancy said to Ben, "I told Flora that Rebekah was pretending to be an angel, not an airplane, and should be commended, not reprimanded."

He looked at her, but she looked away and stubbornly stared at the window. "Is that true?" he asked.

"No."

He was taking all the fun out of what she'd said to Flora and making her feel like a liar now. Nancy paced around, ranting and raving, trying to justify what she'd said, while Ben just sat there rocking gently in his swivel chair, infuriating Nancy further.

Finally, when she ran out of steam, she glared at him.

He looked at her with a spark of amusement in his eyes. "You do make things lively." He rose and went to her and enfolded her in his arms. "I love you," he said.

She couldn't speak as she lay her head against his chest, feeling his heartbeat.

That's when she felt embarrassed about her own shortcomings. Ben knew them better than anyone, made her aware of them, and loved her anyway. "I love you," she said, knowing how good Ben was to her, and for her.

She returned to the sanctuary and called Rebekah over to the piano. "You look more like an angel with wings than an airplane," she said. "Let's see if you can sing like an angel."

Rebekah loved the idea. Nancy played choruses that Rebekah had learned in children's church. Finally, she said, "Let's show Daddy."

"Run get him," Nancy said as Rebekah had already hopped down from the piano bench and ran through the doorway.

Ben came to the door.

"Play," Rebekah urged.

Nancy began to play, expecting Rebekah to hop up on the bench. Instead, she ran up the aisles, waving her arms, "I'm an angel. I'm an angel," and singing her choruses.

Ben came over and stood at the piano where he and Nancy could see Rebekah and yet gaze into each other's faces. "I love you," Ben said. "You have such a beautiful way of atoning."

Nancy was glad she knew the choruses without looking at the keys. Tears pooled in her eyes and ran down her cheeks. "I love you," she said.

The idea had not come from her goodness but from Ben's gentle reprimand and from God's Spirit within.

After a while, Ben said it was noon. They needed to leave for lunch. Church members would be calling or coming in by one o'clock, and he still had work to do on his Sunday sermon.

Ben fastened Rebekah's seat belt in back. Nancy paused a moment with her hand on the car door handle. She looked up and saw a jet plane, a silver glint high in the sky, leaving a line of fast-fading contrail streaking the sky. Then it was gone.

That's what her thoughts of Woody were like. A married woman could remember her life before her husband. But she could not dwell on it, except for its positive impact. Woody had once dreamed of flying. Nancy had dreamed of traveling with him all over the world.

Instead, he'd taken a teaching job. She'd married a preacher.

Both Jim and her mom had said a couple of times that Woody would probably marry. The last time she heard, he hadn't.

The streak of contrail became like puffs of mist in the

sky, fast fading. She allowed one last sentiment before getting into the car.

She hoped Woody was…happy.

Growing drowsy, Nancy reminded herself she had loved Ben with all her heart. Love grew when two people nurtured it. She loved Woody in memory only. They'd never had a life together. She'd had a wonderful life with Ben. She'd learned more by having to immerse herself in the Word of God than she would have flying all over the world.

She had a wonderful daughter. She could never, ever wish for anything different to change that fact. Not another life. Not another child. This was the child of her heart. Rebekah and Ben were her life, along with those she ministered to within the church and in the community.

She knew that losing people she loved in the past had helped condition her for the loss of Ben. Yes, some good came from everything. And each passing day she could see more clearly the good that had come from Ben and his ministry. Her dependence upon the Lord grew stronger. Rebekah had become more dedicated and felt called to the mission field.

She wouldn't tell Woody the details of her life. But the most important one. That, yes, she was a woman of faith. At one time in her life Woody had been number one. She had learned that the greatest need, the greatest love one can have is not another human being but the fulfilling of the Holy Spirit, one's relationship with God and Jesus.

Sometimes she slipped, tried to figure things out for herself. So, her final prayer again committed herself to the Lord to plan her future. She thanked Him for her family.

And her…friends.

Chapter 22

On Tuesday morning, Marge strolled over to the Walkers' right after breakfast. Nancy cleaned the kitchen and slipped into jeans and a navy knit T-shirt. She'd ready herself for the evening later in the day. After making her bed she returned to the living room where her mom and Marge sat reminiscing about the ornaments, taking pictures, and making entries on paper.

"You want to use my laptop?" Nancy offered.

"No," Marge said. "We don't have time to sit on anyone's lap."

They laughed at Nancy's open mouth.

"Just kidding," Marge said. "I do have one of those contraptions. For recipes mainly. I even have a Facebook page. I'm telling you, language has changed. People talk about having hundreds of friends." She shook her head. "Why, they never even met some of them. Thank you kindly, I'll stick with the ones I can see." She pointed at Nancy's mom, and they laughed together.

Nancy was glad those two had been friends so long and lived close to each other. She'd had a few special friends. Cheerleaders when she was one. Roommates in college. Glenda in particular at the hospital. But they'd gone separate ways.

Not wanting to infringe on her mom and Marge's reminiscence with the ornaments and their memories, Nancy returned to the bedroom to sort through the boxes of old books and papers.

She turned back the lids of one and discovered something familiar that felt like a stab in her heart. The journal that she'd begun twenty-five years ago when she was seventeen. The night of her first real kiss. She hadn't been able to sleep that night for being so elated about standing in the arms of the man she loved. She relived the moment over and over and wrote about it on notebook paper.

As soon as she could, she'd purchased a zippered journal with a lock and key. She'd copied from the notebook paper into the journal and relived again that magical night when the snow had fallen and she'd given her heart to Woody Lawing. She had told him of her undying love.

Undying.

She hadn't known then that everything was dying. Nothing on earth lived forever.

But just as she remembered her wonderful life with Ben, and some instances as clearly as if they were happening again, she remembered her childhood, and her single years, just as her mom remembered Tommy in the first grade.

Nancy didn't need to read the account again. A twenty-five-year-old memory could emerge without the slightest provocation. The lock and key had long been lost, but she slowly unzipped the journal, remembering that she'd written on the last page, "I won't write in here again, until Woody says YES."

He hadn't said yes to her proposal.

She might as well throw the journal away. It didn't belong with her memorabilia of Ben where someone like Rebekah or any future grandchildren might happen across it.

But she unzipped it, and her hand touched the first page. The first words she'd written were, "He kissed me."

Nancy's vision blurred from the moisture in her eyes. She felt again how a girl feels when she's *sweet seventeen* and in love. A lifetime ago. Her movement to close the journal revealed something stuck in the middle of it. Nancy opened it and saw a piece of paper on top of an envelope. The envelope had Woodrow Lawing's name on it followed by the European address where she sent letters to him a long time ago.

The fluttering of her heart was not that of a seventeen-year-old in love but of a forty-two-year-old woman whose heart had converted into a drum.

With trembling fingers, she unfolded the sheet of paper and read a hastily scrawled note:

Nancy,

Post office was crowded. Didn't have time to stand in line for a stamp. Had to get Betty to the bus station on time, and you know me, always late. I brought this back, knowing you'd see it since you write in this journal every night. Sorry, but knew you wouldn't want me to take this home with me. I'd probably lose it. Keep in touch.

Marlene

The letter had never been mailed. Woody couldn't respond to something he never received.

What had he thought?

That she had ceased to care about him?

"Oh, Woody, Woody." Nancy pressed the letter to her chest and cried.

He hadn't rejected her. She had kept his letters, cherishing them, until she'd accepted Ben's proposal, and Woody's last words to her had been, "Be happy."

She'd cried when she threw away his letters before marrying Ben. He could no longer be a part of her life. He never had been, except as a friend.

Nancy tried to remember what his last letter had said. He had mentioned love, but she also remembered thinking, after he hadn't responded to her proposal, he had meant he loved her as more than a friend, whatever that meant.

Now she didn't have to feel embarrassed that Woody rejected her proposal. He didn't even know about it.

Why stir up the past?

She was beginning to understand Woody as a young man better, when his dad's support and wishes played a major part in his life. To know him as an accomplished man. And most of all know the Lord had developed a deep faith in him.

She would remain true to her resolve and let him know she was a woman of faith. How her relationship with Ben had inspired and encouraged her to give her life completely to the Lord. Oh, she took it back from time to time, she made her mistakes, she doubted her prayers reached higher than the ceiling at times. But that was momentary. That was the old nature surfacing. She had been forgiven because she had committed her life to Jesus Christ.

Now she recalled the Bible study at church where they discussed what was from God and what was from Satan. After much discussion, they'd concluded that with what we call bad things that happen, if we are close to the Lord, He will use them to produce good and to result in our spiritual growth.

Was this unmailed letter an act of God, or a mistake?

In those moments of contemplation she again committed her life, her future to the Lord and asked that He show her where her home should be, in North Carolina, in Silver City, or in Timbuktu.

That evening, after her mom was ready to pick Marge

up and go to the church meeting, Nancy told her she was going out.

Her mom looked at her for a long moment, but Nancy looked away. When she glanced again her mom was fiddling with an ornament on the tree. "Maybe we'd better not leave the lights on while we're gone." Then she looked at Nancy again. "You do have your key."

Nancy nodded.

"Well, I'd better leave. We don't want to be late."

"Have a good time."

Her mom smiled. "My sentiments exactly." Then she said, "You look happy." Before Nancy thought of a decent reply, her mom left the living room. Then Nancy heard the back door softly close.

Well, she felt happy. The twenty-year burden of feeling rejected no longer existed. She no longer needed to feel uncomfortable with Woody. So, that was settled.

Should she mention the letter to him? Would she cause more discomfort for him? More embarrassment for herself? They couldn't laugh about it, of course. But they could say it was all behind them now and that they can be just…special friends…like the Lawings and the Walkers used to be.

She was no longer that teenager but now a grown woman. But not an old woman by any means. She was still youthful and vibrant…and she was going to look like it. After all, she was a single woman going out to dinner with an old…or rather a former and a new friend.

Yes, this was Christmas, and she would look the part.

He was a very good-looking man and deserved a friend out with him to be complementary.

There was no need to mention the letter.

Yes, common sense said to let it go.

Chapter 23

When his mom was ready to go and waiting for Jean Walker to pick her up, Woody told her, "I'm having dinner at the Knight Hotel. Call if you need me."

"I doubt I will," she said, surprising him. He'd expected her to ask if he was dining alone, but she still respected his having told her years ago he didn't intend to discuss his personal life unless there was something in particular he wanted to tell her.

She simply said, "I'm learning what I can do and can't do. So I don't intend to pick up anything heavier than my Bible."

"What about that?" He pointed to her purse lying on the coffee table.

"That's cute," she chided. "I'll have you know I don't have anything in there heavier than the kitchen sink."

Jean Walker's car pulled into the drive. "Have a good time, Mom."

"You, too. Oh, and don't turn the tree lights on if you're not here."

He opened the door then closed it after her and walked over to the window where the Christmas tree stood, decorated with lights and several ornaments. Others were still in a box, waiting until the women could continue with their project.

He watched his mom get into the car and the excited, happy way the two women greeted each other. After all these years. He was glad for them. He suspected such friendships were rare. His and Jim's had lasted, but it wasn't as close as if he'd had a wife and they could associate as couples. And Woody had been out of the country much of his life.

As he readied for the evening, he wondered how many times he should ask Nancy out to prove to them both he hadn't been, and wasn't, suffering from rejection. And how many times would she accept?

And why *did* she accept?

For the sake of the family?

No. He was still friends with her family. Maybe she wanted to apologize for rejecting him. No, she couldn't do that because it would seem to diminish the life she had with her husband and daughter.

And what would he wear?

He searched in the closet where he'd hung extra clothes he'd brought on Sunday night when he'd come for the Singing Christmas Tree event.

Concern for his attire was as foreign to him as when he'd thought about where to sit. He knew women concerned themselves with how to dress. He'd normally wear slacks, a turtle neck, and a sports coat for a place like the Knight Hotel.

But this was Christmas. And he didn't want to look underdressed as if he were nonchalant about the dinner. A suit. Yes, that would be acceptable even if Nancy had decided this wasn't a dressy occasion. Just…dinner at the hometown hotel.

He decided on the navy suit, the medium-blue shirt that he'd been told accentuated his eye color, as if that mattered. Of course it didn't, but he wore it anyway and chose one of his Christmas ties that had red and green circles on a navy background, and he thought that could represent the season. Maybe give him a youngish look as if he weren't stuffy or anything.

As if that mattered…either.

He settled into the driver's seat, turned the key in the ignition, and let the car warm up while thinking he should have worn the turtleneck. It suited the car better. But he wasn't taking the car to dinner.

Before he could get out and go to the door at the Walker house, Nancy emerged. He did make it to the passenger side of the car by the time she reached it. After all, she was wearing heels, and they weren't low. The long brownish coat fell to just below her knees. She had nice calves. That was just an observation.

Her knees were fine, too, he noted as she got into the car and the edge of the coat fell away. She reached for the coat and covered the sliver of green silk or satin that had shown through. He didn't deliberately peek.

He could admire, just as he noticed or admired a certain color or style of hair, or a pretty face. He could appreciate, but knew the difference between that and ogling.

He wasn't ogling Nancy. He was just…seeing her.

At the reception desk in the foyer, the attendant said, "Just a moment," after Woody gave his name for the reservation. Almost immediately, Thomas Knight came. "Dr. Lawing, welcome." He looked at Nancy. "And I've seen you at church. I believe you're Mrs. Walker's daughter."

Nancy affirmed she was. The three of them spoke briefly about their families, the church, the hotel, then Thomas said, "I've saved two tables." He led the way into the dining room. "Would you prefer the one near the fireplace and Christmas tree or farther over at the window?"

Woody looked at Nancy. She grinned, as if they were both thinking the same thing. *Where to sit?*

"Near the tree and fireplace," she said to Thomas. "Thank you." She moved to where she would face the tree and the fire.

She unbuttoned her coat and began to shrug out of it. Thomas took it and asked if he might drape it over another chair, and she said yes. Woody seated her. Looking at the round table that could easily seat six, Woody decided that sitting opposite her would mean they'd have to talk loudly to be heard if the dining room filled. Not wanting to block her view, he sat at her left.

Perhaps the flames were what gave a shimmer to her dark green dress. The shimmer matched the silver chain with a diamond in the center that circled her neck and lay against her smooth skin below her throat.

Thomas took their napkins and laid them across their laps.

"Owner *and* waiter tonight?" Woody asked.

Thomas laughed lightly. "Occasionally. For special patrons." He added with emphasis, "Particularly of the arts."

"My mom loves your paintings, too." Nancy lifted her hand. "She said you painted the ones in here."

"Yes, feel free to look."

"I'd like to."

Thomas smiled at her then nodded at a waiter who came over. "Treat them well, Blackston. They're my special guests. Soup's on the house."

"Yes, sir. Mr. Thomas's famous she-crab soup makes the soul purr like a kitten."

"Now you know why Blackston is headwaiter." Thomas turned to leave. "Enjoy your evening."

Blackston's smile faded, and he resumed the professional stance of a dignified waiter. He named their specials then put the menus before them and took their drink orders.

Nancy's face turned toward the spacious dining room. Her dark eyes seemed to reflect the season, aglow with light, reminding him of her younger years when they shone with excitement and wonder. Now she glanced at him, and they were guarded, like people's were when they felt unsure of something or someone.

She smiled. "Thanks for bringing me here. It's very elegant and beautiful."

He could have said that described her. Instead, he glanced at the white tablecloths with gold fringe. The poinsettia arrangements in the center of the tables. The huge crystal chandeliers. The paintings.

A waitress brought their drinks. After a few sips, Woody asked if she would like to see the paintings, and she said yes. A few other patrons were looking at them.

Woody thought about the times he and a single, mature female were paired for special events by friends or colleagues. He'd finally gained the reputation of being a confirmed bachelor but a decent escort. He'd asked a single art teacher to attend Thomas's exhibit, wanting to understand more about style.

Now he could mention a few things he'd learned as he and Nancy studied the paintings. They returned to the table, and Woody asked, "You know about the famous soup?"

"Mom mentioned Thomas has brought it to the attention of the public again, like it was years ago when it was his grandmother's secret recipe." She smiled. "I suppose I took it and the verse on the menu for granted. I can appreciate it now."

Woody nodded and read aloud from the front of the menu, "'Man does not live by bread alone. He needs soup, too.'"

He turned to the back where the rest of the verse was printed and again read aloud, "'Man shall not live by bread alone, but by every word of God. Luke four, verse four. King James Version.'"

Blackston brought the soup. The elegant soup bowls looked like wide, shallow teacups with two handles. He set them on matching saucers.

Nancy looked askance at hers.

"If you don't like it—"

"No," she said. "I'm worried. He said this makes you purr like a kitten. He didn't know my kittens. They could be worse than Sophie."

Woody gave a short laugh. Yes, that was Nancy. Then he smiled at her. "Shall we pray?"

She nodded, and he said a brief prayer, including blessings for Thomas and all who worked at the hotel. He thanked God for having answered his and Nancy's prayers about his mom and that she was recovering. He thanked God for the food. When he said amen, so did Nancy, and they picked up their spoons.

Their comments were primarily about the best soup either had ever tasted, but going on inside Woody continued a silent prayer that God would restore him and Nancy to a comfortable association. But then it occurred to him the association had not been comfortable since she was seventeen, and—

Ah, Blackston was approaching with a huge round tray balanced on one hand above his shoulder.

As they ate, the conversation turned to places they'd lived. Nancy's eyes glowed as he talked about Europe, and she couldn't seem to hear enough about Paris.

She told him about the beauty of the North Carolina mountains and how Southerners really were among the most hospitable people she'd ever known. "Other than in Silver City," she added.

He didn't know much about North Carolina. "Small-town atmosphere," he said.

The conversation turned to family and his infrequent visits with Jim and his family over the years.

"I always enjoyed seeing his children," he said. "Each time I visited, or the few times they visited at my condo, they seemed to have grown. Not inches, but feet."

"Oh, they really do grow like weeds," she said. "It seems like only yesterday Rebekah was just a little girl. And now she expects to get an official marriage proposal when she and Don are here for Christmas."

She raised her hand up to the table, and he saw her ring spark with light. "Speaking of marriage, Rebekah called this afternoon and confirmed that she and Don would be honored to accept my offer of giving her my wedding rings. They consider it a gift from Ben, too."

She would take off her rings? "I'm sure that's generous of you."

"Yes," she said softly, looking at the rings. "These symbolize our marriage, our commitment to each other. But they're also symbols of that union that gave life to Rebekah. I think this reminder of the kind of man Ben was will be more helpful to *her* now. What Ben was and is to me is in my heart, not on my hand. To Rebekah, this is a reminder of her parents and what we stood for and believed in."

Woody marveled at her attitude. She lowered her hand to her lap, and when she looked at him her eyes were filled with tenderness. "Don is being very generous to understand what these symbols mean to Rebekah. I think it takes a more mature person to do that than to say he must be the one to buy a ring and it must come from him."

"He sounds like a fine young man."

She nodded. "Both of them have heard Ben say many times, don't get caught up in planning a wedding, but consider the lifetime of marriage. He set the example."

Woody smiled. He was glad she'd had a good man and had a wonderful daughter. "Sounds like those young people had terrific parents."

The way she opened her mouth and lifted her eyebrows he thought she was about to refute the fact that she had been terrific. So he drew her attention to what he had to say. "I think I'd make a much better grandparent than a parent," he said honestly. "I have missed not having children. But in another way, I've been blessed. I had time to mentor college students, and taking a group to Europe meant getting close to them. I felt keenly my responsibility of being a Christian example."

"I can imagine you are a good one," Nancy said. "You were that when I was a college student."

He looked over at her again. "I was almost always aware of the difference in our ages."

"I know. In those days, our ages made no difference to me."

"But as you grew older," he said, "you apparently saw the wisdom in my restraint. When I thought you might be adult enough for a different response from me, you had already gone your own way."

She shook her head. "No, I never doubted my feelings for you, until I was rejected by you."

"Rejected?"

She nodded.

He shook his head. "You're the one who rejected me. Remember?"

He watched her put her fork down and lower her hands below the table. She was chewing, but she was looking around, uncomfortably. Perhaps it was because a couple had passed by and spoke to him.

Another couple he thought he had seen at church spoke to Nancy. Was she afraid there'd be talk? Would that be so terrible? They were single. He had not thought of embarrassing her in public. But to take her into DC or out of town might seem like hiding, and he'd certainly not want to give that impression.

"What is it, Nancy?"

She swallowed, took a sip of her drink. Then she said, "I'm thinking before I act or speak."

He thought her as adorable as she was when young and impulsive. But he dared not laugh as if anything were humorous. He enjoyed her. But now he felt the return of the discomfort he'd had before they'd become reacquainted. He took a bite of food. A small one so he might not have difficulty swallowing should she remind him he'd rejected, or seemed to have rejected, her so many times it had finally been one too many times.

He could handle it. He already had. For over twenty years in fact. They were mature adults and could discuss the past with intelligence and objectivity. And that's why he said, "How are you doing with your thinking?"

Chapter 24

Nancy sighed. "It's not working."

She reached over for her purse, and he wondered if she'd decided to leave. Then she removed an envelope and returned the purse to the other chair. "This belongs to you." She held it out to him.

The candle in the center of the red poinsettias flickered as if it might go out.

He took the envelope. On it was his name and his address in Europe, years ago. He looked at her quizzically. "It's sealed."

She nodded. "It's been sealed for over twenty years."

In a thin tone she related the incident of having written it, giving it to Marlene to mail, then finding it and Marlene's note earlier in the day.

"Should I...open it?"

The soft material shimmered on her shoulder as she lifted it in a light shrug. "That's up to you. It was my response to your last letter many years ago."

Woody felt like he was on the ball field, running, and was tackled around his feet, and there was nothing to do but fall face-first. He might fall forward into his plate, and he wasn't wearing a helmet.

Her response?

This was her response to the letter when he'd indicated, he was sure, although he didn't recall exactly what he'd written, that he did love her and was ready for a commitment?

He needed time to think. She said thinking hadn't worked for her. He had a strong feeling it wasn't going to work for him either.

He stared at the envelope. If her response had been that she'd met someone else, he could…yes, he could say the past twenty-something years have shown that.

If her response was that she had still loved him, he could… yes, say the mistake worked to her benefit because the past twenty-something years have shown that.

He laid the blue envelope on the table. The table knife lay across the edge of his plate. Should he take his napkin and wipe the greasy stains of butter from it?

Looking across at Nancy's plate he saw her knife was doing the same as his. He would feel silly wiping the knife. And, too, it might stain the envelope. Or he might drop it and stain his pants. Did Nancy know he'd be nervous about this? Maybe. Perhaps she wanted him to suffer.

Looking around, he saw Blackston who looked his way, so Woody nodded slightly to indicate he needed help. Blackston came. "Could I have a clean knife, please?"

A horrified look crossed Blackston's face. "I'm so sorry. Is something—"

"No." Woody felt worse. He was making a scene. He should have said he'd open it later. But if she had wanted him to open it later she would have given it to him later. "I would like a clean table knife so I can open this envelope."

Blackston's face relaxed. He moved to the closest unoccupied table, took a knife, and handed it to Woody. "Anything else?"

Woody looked at Nancy. "Dessert?"

Blackston filled the silence by naming desserts. Nancy said, "Bananas Foster would be delightful."

"The same," Woody said. Dessert seemed like such a foreign thing at the moment. But they had come here for dinner.

Maybe the Christmas lights or the candlelight were reflected in Nancy's eyes, but he got a feeling she was enjoying his apparent discombobulating preparation for opening an envelope.

Well…he needed to be careful. The letter was almost an antique.

Just as he managed to get the knife into the corner of the envelope she said, "You can wait if you want to."

He couldn't help but say, "Seems I've already done that."

After he wiggled the edge of the knife into the unglued space, reminding him of his own threatening condition, he managed to slit the top without harming himself. He laid the knife down, took out the blue stationery, and unfolded the page. Lacy snowflakes were falling around a jolly white snowman with an orange carrot nose, black eyes, black top hat, and scarf. There were pink lip prints. He blinked to clear his eyes and focus on the writing.

My dearest Woody,

I know you think I'm impulsive, and you're right. But I've thought about this all day, after having thought about it for as long as I can remember. Your last letter meant more than I can say. There is only one possible response I can make.

I have always loved you. I always will.

WILL YOU MARRY ME?
Yours "truly" forever!
Nancy

He thought he was prepared. He had expected her continued declaration of love. But to propose? Well, yes. That was
Nancy. Back then.

Who was Nancy now?

Who was he?

Different. And the same.

He lowered the letter to his legs and held it there. He didn't
want her to see his hands shake. No, not his hands. He felt
much like you do when swimming and for an instant you don't
move and you feel the ripples caress you, or when struck by a
strong wind and the force threatens to knock you off your feet.

He heard a sound. Blackston came with a cart. Woody stared
as Blackston began the flambeau process for the bananas Foster. There was the mixture. Then the flames. They burned
higher, and he heard Nancy say, "I love to watch that."

Good. That's what he needed to do.

Then the flames burned lower as the alcohol burned off.
Blackston dished the mixture into small crystal goblets of ice
cream and set the desserts before them. Woody picked up his
spoon and tasted, aware of the hot and the cold sensations.
Blackston waited. Woody nodded. Nancy said, "Perfect."

Blackston went away.

"I just wanted you to know," Nancy said, "especially after
you said I rejected you, that I didn't." Her voice was thin, maybe
from the ice cream. "I thought you didn't answer my proposal
because you'd told me so many times that we were just friends,
and I thought you didn't want to embarrass me further."

Then it dawned on him. For over twenty years she'd
thought he'd not answered her proposal. That astonished him.
"You thought I received the letter and ignored it?" he said
with amazement.

"Well, no. Not ignored. I thought you were tired of telling
me. Had to do something to knock some sense into me. Not
responding"—she smiled faintly—"did it."

He took a bite, not that he tasted it. He just knew it was

something to do. Something hot or cold. He shook his head. "You should not have assumed I hadn't responded. I'd never done that before."

His eyes met hers then. Her eyes flashed. Dark brown with little golden flecks. Like the old, or rather the young Nancy. The girl was…still in there. "What else could I think?" Her dress shimmered with her deep intake of breath and the squaring of her shoulders. Her chin lifted slightly to the side.

He stared at her. She was waiting. Why did she do this? To torture him? What was going on inside her? Was she trying to make him comfortable. Or uncomfortable?

"Well?" she said.

He let his gaze move toward the fireplace, toward the tree. He couldn't figure it out. He was known for being able to think on his feet. He had to do that with college students. But they posed a challenge in which he could be objective. Fortunately he wasn't on his feet now, but sitting. And this was…Nancy. What to say?

He couldn't help but laugh. "That's not a funny laugh," he informed her. "An ironic one. We both thought we were rejected by the other."

"I still don't know if I was," she said. "Because I don't know how you would have reacted if you had gotten my proposal."

He became conscious of voices, heard the clink of silverware, glimpsed movement, smelled the aroma of food, saw the colors of Christmas, became aware of a shimmery green dress; his heart was full, but his brain was empty.

"Well?" she prompted.

"I'm…thinking."

Her impatient gaze lifted toward the ceiling for a moment before she settled into the bananas Foster. He had a feeling their roles had reversed. He'd always been the one to wait until the time was right, was better, to prepare, plan. Now she seemed strong, able to handle her own life, not dependent on what he wanted but had her own reasonable, mature way of making decisions.

He had never needed to woo her. She'd always been there, wooing him. Frightening him? What if she was too young? What if he couldn't support her? What if he failed his dad, his parents? What if her young, free spirit became dwarfed by work and putting his plans first, and abandonment of herself? Had he been afraid?

Fear not. Fear not. Fear not. He could almost hear the heavenly host singing, *"Fear not: for, behold, I bring you good tidings of great joy."*

No, Dr. Lawing, you are not the impulsive one. Have never been.

He watched her concentrate on the dessert.

This was the Nancy he knew and didn't know.

Who is this Nancy now? What does he know of her? He knows her background. He knows her as a child, as a girl, as a teen, as a young woman. He knows she brought a snow globe into a hospital room and a man she thought rejected her was sitting there. She prayed for his mom.

She is devoted to God and family and her daughter. She had been hurt by him and yet is associating with him. She is not bitter. She is forgiving. She has borne many trials. She is open and honest. She is trying to be comfortable, accepting, a friend. If he had not known her in the past, he knew enough about her now to be convinced she was a beautiful woman in every way.

He sat there staring at her, not eating his own dessert. He held a spoon and had no idea if he looked like he gripped a baton and was leading a band—perhaps he was, because he felt as if a marching band were inside him—or a drum anyway. He guided the spoon into the crystal goblet and scooped a bite.

"Is it working?"

He looked over at her. "What?"

"Your thinking." Her voice held a hint of exasperation.

"It's beginning to." He decided to smile, or grin at least.

Her shoulders lifted. "Don't you want to say what you would have done if you'd received the letter? I mean, just to make sure we're clear on everything."

He deliberately drew his eyebrows together. "I've decided," he said, "since I received the letter more than twenty years after it was written, I should wait more than twenty years before telling you what I would have said or done."

He spooned into the last of his dessert then glanced over at her.

Her mouth was open, and she was breathing more heavily.

She reminded him of Sophie when she lifted her chin, had finished the dessert, and moved the goblet aside. He didn't want her sashaying from the dining room. "However, on second thought—"

Blackston was coming. "Coffee?"

"Yes."

"Two coffees with cream," he said to Blackston.

He watched her. She looked off and smiled, apparently at someone at another table.

She waited, impatiently, but waited. Blackston brought the coffee.

"All right," she said, now that the coffee was before them. "How would you have responded?"

Now that he'd had a few minutes to absorb this and think, he leaned forward. "You have just surprised me with a letter written over twenty years ago."

"A proposal," she corrected.

He acknowledged that with a slight nod. "If you will allow me, I want to respond as I would have twenty years ago."

She nodded.

He tucked the envelope into his suit coat pocket then picked up his cup. When he returned it to the table she said, "Well?"

"Well what?"

"You were going to tell me what you would have said or done. Since you said you wouldn't have let it go unanswered."

"No, I said I would respond the way I would have over twenty years ago. I couldn't have gotten back to you instantly."

"You'd have had to think about it."

He lifted a hand. "Don't put words in my mouth. This ball is in my court, so to speak. Let me do this my way."

Only a minute flash of gold sparked her dark eyes, then they took on an expression he'd seen in many a college girl that seemed to mean "whatever."

Yes, Nancy was no longer pursuing him. She was a woman strong enough to make it on her own. He knew of only one thing lacking in her life.

And that was knowing where to sit.

Chapter 25

Sitting beside Woody on the dark leather seat, Nancy reminded herself this was not twenty-plus years ago. Woody could play that game, but she mustn't. And yet, she had a rather giddy feeling as he drove along, down the main street and even a few side streets, and they talked about the decorations and laughed about things and people and events from the past.

Well, why wouldn't she feel a little giddy? This *was* silly, wasn't it? At least Woody wasn't running from her. Not that she was chasing anymore. When they arrived home, she said, "Don't get out."

Not that he would have. This wasn't a date. And if he did get out and walk her to the door what would they do? Shake hands?

"I'll be in touch," he said. "As I would have twenty-some years ago, remember?"

"Good night." She laughed lightly then strode, just as lightly, up the walkway and into the house. Twenty-five years ago they wouldn't have gone to dinner, not unless with a group, and she wouldn't have been in a car alone with him unless it was a necessity or emergency. And in those days she would have been proclaiming her love for him.

Seeing the Christmas tree lights on, she knew her mom was home. Just then she came into the room. "Let me change, Mom. Then we can talk."

After they donned their nightclothes, her mom surprised her by not asking anything personal. They talked about the church meeting and the dinner at the hotel.

The most her mom said about Woody was that Marge appreciated his staying with her. She was improving but still shouldn't lift anything heavy or move around too much. He had even taken over most of the cooking, was replacing burned-out lightbulbs, and was helping get rid of things in the basement she tended to accumulate but didn't need. He kept the tree stand filled with water.

"Sophie's beginning to accept him," she said.

Nancy thought of that later. She, too, was beginning to accept him as the mature man he had become. This game he was playing reminded her of the young Woody before she had scared him with her obsessive love.

She'd already had over twenty years of feeling rejected, so his saying it now wouldn't hurt as much as it did then. Now, she expected it. He would think about it. Find a kind, reassuring way to tell her.

He wanted to respond like he would have years ago.

Okay.

She'd wait.

Patiently.

And she lay awake a long, long time. Waiting. Patiently. Until she forced her thoughts to her precious daughter and Don who would soon be on their way back from their week in Honduras. She prayed. That always made her sleepy.

The next morning she was eating breakfast when her mom's landline rang.

Her mom hurried out of her chair to answer. "Oh, I hope nothing's wrong. Nobody calls this early. Hello?" she said. Then, "Is Marge all right. Oh. Yes."

She handed the phone to Nancy. "Hello?"

"Nancy," he said. "This is Woody. I hoped you'd still be home. It's eleven thirty here in London. So it should be around seven thirty there. Just to let you know, I got your letter. I decided to come home for Christmas after all. We'll talk." A pause. "Okay?"

She breathed in.

"You there?"

She breathed out. "Um." She cleared her throat and felt her eyes stuck on her mom and her mom's seemed stuck, too. "We may have a bad connection from all the way across the ocean. But…" *Oh my goodness.* She giggled. "Okay." She would not have giggled back then, even though she was young. Maybe she was entering that proverbial second childhood. No, this wasn't childish. It was…what?

"Bye, then," he said.

She heard the click. She hadn't said bye. She held the phone out to her mom who took it, rose from her seat again, walked over to the wall, and hung it up.

"Oh, I'm sorry," Nancy said. "I should have done that."

"Well, I can see you're in some kind of state. Is something wrong?"

"I don't know," Nancy said. "Did I say 'okay'?"

Her mom nodded.

So Nancy nodded.

"What's going on?"

Nancy shook her head. "I don't really know."

She didn't. What had gotten into him? That wasn't the Woody she knew. But he said he'd respond the way he would have over twenty years ago. She'd always taken the initiative in their one-sided relationship. He was always so sensible. He wouldn't have acted like that. But, he said he was coming home for Christmas.

What in the world did *that* mean? Would he have flown in the next day? Would he have a thesis to finish first? A class? She thought he'd also been an assistant to a professor in the master's program. Come home the *week* before Christmas? The *day* before?

Okay, what would she have done back then? She would have wanted to again express her undying love. But to come right out and write a proposal made it different. And if he had called and said they'd talk, she would have backed away, being afraid of what he might say, of ruining her life forever.

Yet, she would have waited. He'd said, *"We'll talk."*

But this was really just a silly game. He was being playful. Maybe those college students had taught him to loosen up. But she was sensible now. The game would have to end. Mainly because she had no choice. She had her daughter and Don to think about. She'd pick them up at the airport. They'd…talk.

Woody called the day after Rebekah and Don arrived. He said he saw the car and who he thought would be Rebekah and again offered to take them into DC. Nancy talked it over with Rebekah and Don, who were eager to accompany Woody into DC. She called Woody back.

They set up the time for the following morning. "Just so you know," Woody said. "Twenty-plus years ago, I'm not back from London yet."

Nancy managed to say, "Okay." This time without choking on her saliva. They could laugh. They could relate. He couldn't say anything worse than what she'd thought for the past twenty years. And it didn't matter now anyway. That was…over twenty years ago, and they were becoming friends as mature adults. That's what she was now. Absolutely.

Okay!

Don had the guest room and Rebekah slept with Nancy.

She did one of Rebekah's favorite things and rubbed her sweet daughter's back until she went to sleep. Nancy loved sleeping with her warm, precious daughter. They had not slept together in many years. In the garage apartment, Rebekah slept on the couch until she moved into the dorm at UNCA.

The next morning, Woody drove Nancy's car, and they left early. "I want you to see the sun rise over the obelisk," he said, and thus became the professor as Nancy imagined him teaching those college students.

Woody spoke with authority, knowledge, and faith as he talked about the beacon that rose 555 feet over the District of Columbia's sixty-nine square miles. He spoke of the White House, the Lincoln Memorial, the Capitol, and the Jefferson Memorial, but the obelisk was a tribute and testimony to God.

He talked about the aluminum capstone and the two words carved into it.

Laus Deo.

"It means 'Praise be to God,'" he explained.

Nancy watched the two young people look at Woody and the obelisk with wonder and sunshine on their faces. She remembered Woody saying his testimony was his accountability. Yes, she could see that. He began his tour with a testimony to his faith in God, a reminder or a lesson on the faith America was founded on, great men who stood for what they believed, why and how America became a great nation. He said it's like a person. One who puts his life in the hands of Jesus Christ and follows Him is a part of the laus Deo.

"But you two know that." He turned to the young people. "I understand you're planning to go into mission work."

"We know," Don agreed. "But we also know we're just beginning. It's encouraging to see people like you and Rebekah's mom and know about the years you've been faithful to the Lord."

Nancy felt the sun in her eyes but didn't think that's why they became moist. She could not think of a better compliment from a young person. She had not been as consciously committed to the Lord when she was Don's and Rebekah's ages. She'd taken her faith for granted. Years of maturity had deepened it.

"Thank you," Woody said, and Nancy thought he was probably thinking much the same as she, that many years had been lived apart from a complete surrender to the Lord.

Looking up at the obelisk was the perfect beginning to a day, like having a devotional and spending time with laus Deo. Woody took them past the World War II and Vietnam Memorials and spoke of self-sacrifice, nobility, bravery, love for God and country.

He obviously knew these young people didn't want a tour of historic places right now. When he asked, they wanted to know about some of the more familiar places and recent events. What had the national christmas Tree lighting been like? Had he gone? He had.

They wanted to see Georgetown University and where Woody lived.

He drove through Georgetown and warned them. "It's a combination of historic and trendy," he told them. "But be aware. We have exploding manhole covers in Washington, most of them in Georgetown." He explained about underground electrical cables frayed for various reasons, sometimes rats, that mix with gasses and ignite.

He also told of the writers who had lived in Georgetown, writers that included Sinclair Lewis, Archibald MacLeish, Francis Scott Key, and Louisa May Alcott.

As they neared his home, he pointed out the Kennedy Center. They loved his home and its view of the Potomac River.

At one point Don said, "It's been said that we're not a Christian nation." He looked at Woody and stretched out his hand. "Thanks to you, Dr. Lawing, I know it is."

Nancy could tell that Woody was emotionally moved. He said thanks, and the two men, yes, she saw Don as a man, shook hands. Rebekah smiled at Nancy. This was Don's first trip to DC.

Rebekah had visited DC and Silver City many times and had seen some of the sights, since Jim lived not that far away in Virginia. But she knew her daughter, along with her cousins Stephen and Carol, had mainly been interested in summertime fun and the malls.

Woody took them to Tony & Joe's Seafood Place for supper. They sat at an outdoor table where they enjoyed a spectacular view of the Potomac. She and Woody ate flatbread pizza right along with the young couple.

When he suggested they take the metro and see the lighting of the national tree at dusk, they were all delighted. They were enthralled with the huge tree and its lights. Nancy lifted her gaze, even higher than the obelisk, and praised God for the blessing of her family. And friends.

On the way back to Silver City, Rebekah and Don talked about their recent and former trips to Honduras. Several natives had accepted the Lord, and a church was almost finished. They'd put in some hard work during the past week.

Woody asked Rebekah about her North Carolina life. She told him about the university, the beauty of the mountains, and she raved about the Biltmore Estate and said he must see it. He said he was sorry she had lost her dad.

Rebekah talked about Ben, about his being such a wonderful dad and preacher. "He wasn't just a dad. He was the best Christian example I've ever known. He always knew what to say. Oops. No offense. What I mean is, Mom fussed; Dad preached."

But then Nancy felt Rebekah's hand on her shoulder. She looked back to see her girl had leaned forward. Nancy reached up and laid her hand on Rebekah's. "Kidding, sort of," Rebekah said.

"I know," Nancy said. She wanted Rebekah's memories of her dad to be only positive. And Ben's life had made that easy.

Woody looked over and smiled.

After Woody drove Nancy's car into the Walker carport, he said he'd walk the few steps home. Rebekah watched him walk down the driveway and onto the sidewalk. "He's wonderful, Mom," she said.

Nancy nodded. "Obviously the kind of teacher that's needed to remind young people what our nation was, is, and should be."

"I think he's just a really nice person. Good-looking, too."

Don opened the back door and held it open for them to enter. They went into the kitchen. Her mom said on the phone, "Nancy and Rebekah are here now. All right. Bye." She hung up. "That was Jim," she said. "Now, let's sit down and you two tell me all about it."

They sat at the kitchen table for a while with goodies, and Rebekah did most of the telling, and her grandmother loved every minute of it. They simply hadn't seen each other enough during the past years, although they were always together at Christmas, at some point during the summer, and often at special occasions. They'd had busy lives, like everyone.

Nancy remembered when Rebekah had returned from a visit to Jim's. She talked about Stephen having gone on the European tour with Woody's group. Rebekah had said she wanted to go to Georgetown when she started college. Nancy would not allow that. Out-of-state tuition was one thing. But not the only thing. They did not need the contact of Woody being her history professor, nor of her going to Europe with him for the summer.

As one would expect of a girl in love, Rebekah began to talk about Don and mentioned the rings. "Sure you don't mind, Mom?"

Nancy touched her wedding rings. She shook her head. "What's in my heart and mind remains, even if these aren't on my finger."

She took them off, and her hand flexed as if it felt strange, rather naked without the rings.

"I know how you feel," Nancy's mom said. She fingered the necklace she wore almost all the time. She'd had a heart made from her wedding band, and the diamond hung in the center of it. She'd said that was what she wanted to do instead of wearing them on her finger after her husband died. "My hand felt strange," she said. "But you're right. And this will be yours someday, Nancy."

Nancy nodded and handed the rings to Rebekah. "You really don't mind that you will wear these instead of one that Don would get for you?"

"We both think this is more special, Mom. Why buy a ring when I can have a part of Dad on my finger. It will be sort of like he's at the wedding, too. And in our lives. Don loved Dad. He feels this is an honor." Tears sprang into her eyes. "I do, too."

They hugged and wiped their faces. Yes, Nancy understood that a young girl in love was most concerned about being in the life of her beloved. They, like everyone in life, would face their difficulties, but they were blessed to be starting out with the right attitudes and with their greatest desire to serve the Lord.

It wasn't until late when Nancy was dozing that her thoughts went again to Woody. She saw him in action as Dr. Lawing. She saw him as an example and teacher of young people. She saw him as generous, accommodating, energetic, friends with her family, with her. He was an accomplished man, one of faith. And as Rebekah had said, good-looking, too.

She was seeing him as the mature man instead of as the fanciful dream of her youth, when nothing in life really mattered but him. Now she was more practical, more realistic.

But despite herself, as if this were over twenty years ago, she wondered when in the world he would arrive from Europe. And…talk.

Chapter 26

Nancy decided it wasn't such a good idea after all for her to be left in that state of what became anxiety. She would like to know how he would have reacted, but it changed nothing. They had lived separate lives and that was that.

When she saw him she would simply say he could tell her or not. Her past feelings for him were too real to be playing games like this. She welcomed the arrival of Jim, Lauren, Stephen, and Carol. The household was busy and joyful. Except for the afternoon when Jim and his family left to take their bags to the Knight Hotel where they would stay for several days. Jim, Lauren, and Carol would have an adjoining room to Stephen and Don. They were all eager to get better acquainted with Don and make him part of the family.

The afternoon before Christmas Eve, Nancy was alone in the house. Jim and Lauren were having dinner at the hotel with friends they had in Silver City. The young people went out to find their own kind of food place. That evening, the family would have refreshments and play games.

Nancy's mom went down to the Lawings to help Marge pack up some goodies she would bring for the get-together that evening.

Nancy, her mom, and Lauren had made cookies, candies, cheese and cracker trays, and vegetable trays during the morning. The afternoon was overcast. Nancy didn't want her attitude to reflect the gloom so she showered, washed her hair, and dressed in a red silk blouse for a festive look. Wearing it with black denims gave a casual look. She slipped into black high-heeled sandals and was just fastening shiny gold loops at her ears when the doorbell rang.

Ah, just about family time. She hurried to the door and there he stood. She stared while he huddled beneath his jacket. The wind played havoc with his hair. He had that look on his face she remembered, as if he were about to say something she'd rather not hear.

"Cold out here," he said.

She almost said he was early. The family hadn't arrived. Her mom was at…his house.

Oh!

Did this mean he was playing that game of having just arrived from London? At first, it had seemed like a good idea. But now, she really didn't want to hear it.

He opened the screen, so she stepped back. He came in and closed the door. "You look beautiful." He pulled off his leather jacket. He was wearing a cream-colored turtleneck and jeans.

She reached for his jacket, but he said, "I'll just lay it here over the chair."

That meant he wouldn't be staying long. So he had not come for the evening of family and longtime friends gathering to eat and play games and enjoy Christmas together.

"So do you," she said.

His eyes questioned, then realization sparked in them that she was referring to the "beautiful" remark. His fingers tried to brush his hair back into place. She liked it in disarray and remembered she had tried tousling it one time, so long ago, but he had taken her hand from his hair. So, she wouldn't do it now.

She'd learned.

"Would you…have a seat?" he said.

She had a vague idea *she* should have said that. After all, he was a guest, no, a friend, in the Walker home.

She looked around. She wouldn't sit in that chair because his jacket was on it. Not the couch because she didn't want to act like she thought he'd sit beside her. She sat in an easy chair. She was warm enough so she didn't need to get any closer to the fire. The Christmas tree lights were on. The room felt cozy.

For now, she would hear him telling her why he could not accept her proposal and vow she meant more than a friend. She would say thank you. They would be friends over the holidays. Then she would get herself back to the mountains of North Carolina where she belonged and hibernate like a bear.

She would reappear in spring and plan a wedding for her daughter and then look forward to being a grandmother. Yes, her life sounded like a good one.

Indeed.

"Maybe I should apologize to you again," he said.

"No apology needed. We've learned to be friends again. I think we're doing all right, don't you?"

"Not really," he said. "My apology is not for the past but for saying let me respond the way I would have back then. But, I was shocked when you gave me that letter. I couldn't laugh it off. I had felt you rejected me and moved on. When I read your proposal I realized you hadn't rejected me but thought I rejected you."

"I know it was a shock. That's how I felt when I discovered the letter was never mailed." Oh, she just wanted to get this over with. "Just tell me you would have come home from London after all and made clear once and for all we weren't meant for each other."

He shook his head. "No, Nancy. My last letter to you might not have been clear. But it was preliminary to a proposal. I didn't want to do it on paper, but in person. I loved you, Nancy. It frightened me at first. I told myself all the things I told you, about age, commitment, being sure, becoming prepared, being ready. I even refused to believe what we felt for each other was the lifetime kind of thing. I wasn't ready for lifetime. What commitment to you would mean. Perhaps you were more mature than I, although you were younger."

He had loved her?

She shook her head. "I was impulsive, aggressive, ridiculous."

"No. You were beautiful and wonderful. And you still are. Even more so. But, let me get back to the past. I would have fulfilled my obligations in London as much as I could, then I would have come home for Christmas. I would have asked your dad's permission. I would have given you a ring."

Nancy didn't know if she could stand this. He would have proposed? He had finally been ready? Was she really ready back then to be the kind of wife he would have wanted, needed? She couldn't know. She only knew she'd been the best wife for Ben and best mother for Rebekah that she knew how to be.

But this was good to know. She felt a great relief. Learning he hadn't received the letter only had been partial relief. She thought for a long moment. "I would have accepted that proposal," she said. "But I can't at all regret my marriage to Ben."

"No, I wouldn't expect that. I don't regret it for you. I'm glad for you. That you had a good life and you have a wonderful daughter." He smiled.

"Strange," she said. "In the past few days you and I have tried to be friends again. I think…now, we can."

But he was shaking his head. "No," he said to her surprise. "We can't."

She didn't know what to say, how to question, how to reply.

He took a deep breath, and she heard the shaky release of it. "You remember that tie I wore the evening we had dinner at the hotel?"

"How could I forget?"

He acknowledged that with a slight turn of his head and a grin, in spite of the embarrassed look on his face. "Okay, so I pick out atrocious ties. But after that dinner, when I took it off at home, I looked at those red and green circles. They reminded me of a traffic light. Stop or go. I decided to go. I'm going to be impulsive."

She shook her head. "You're not impulsive. You'd never go on red."

"Not in the past. But this is the present. This is my last chance. I'll go, until you say stop."

Whatever did he mean?

He went over to his jacket, and she wondered if she was supposed to say stop, don't go. But he took something from his jacket pocket. A small bag. He turned to her again. "Like I said, years ago I would have asked your dad's permission. This time I asked Jim's, and he gave it. I would continue with this regardless, but I wanted to know his feelings. He gave his blessing."

Nancy couldn't take her eyes from the bag. He reached in and brought out a little black box, and then he did the strangest thing. He knelt down on one knee. "I loved you then. I love you now. I'm proposing, Nancy. As I would have back then. I love who and what you were all your life. I love you now, in the present. I want to live the rest of my life showing you that I love you."

He opened the box and took out a lovely white-gold ring. "This belongs on that finger," he said. "I know I may be twenty years too late. But I don't want you to have any doubt that I loved you even when I wasn't sure. That I love you now, and I am sure."

"You don't really know me," she whispered.

"I know enough. And I want to learn more."

She took a deep breath. He was waiting. A strange sound escaped her throat. "Where is that girl who, if this happened twenty years ago, would have flung herself at you and suffocated you with kisses?"

"And now?" he said. "You reject me? I deserve that."

"Dr. Lawing," she said, feeling that seventeen-year-old threatening. "If I'd never met you before, I could easily fall in love with you. But I've known you, I've loved you completely, and I love you now. Yes," she said and held out her hand.

He slipped the ring on. It fit perfectly. "This can be exchanged if you—"

"No," she said. "It's perfect."

He rose from his kneeling position, still holding her hand. She looked up at him. He looked worried. She said, "I haven't flung myself at you in a long time, so I don't know—"

He said, "I think we should seal this with a kiss. I haven't done that in a long time."

She said, feeling that seventeen-year-old girl acting up inside again, "You teach history. I'll teach kissing."

He looked more worried, but his blue eyes danced. She reached up and touched his face. His head bent for their lips to meet. The kiss was warm and tender then deep and demanding.

He pulled away, taking a deep breath. "I'm beginning to remember. And it was never as wonderful as this." He touched her lips with his fingers. Then he raised her fingers to his lips and kissed them. "I'm overwhelmed."

She shrugged. "And we've only just begun."

He stepped away, as if scared. "Oh, I have another present for you." He went to his jacket again and removed a package wrapped in snowman paper. Holding it, he said, "I got this idea from Sophie."

"How romantic," she said with playful sarcasm.

He laughed. "No, there's a point here. I discovered the

way to win a woman's heart is to find out what she wants and give it to her. Sophie likes bacon treats. That won her over."

"Oh, and in that little box is a bacon treat for me?"

"Worked with Sophie." He handed it to her. She opened it.

"Oh," she exclaimed, as she took out a little replica of a Victorian chair.

"Since that's something you wanted, I thought it might win you over. It's to remind you," he said, "where you should sit. By my side. Always. That vacant side of my fireplace is where you can put any chair you want. Wherever we go, wherever we live will be up to you. But your place is sitting by my side."

She held the chair gently in the palm of her hand, her fingers cradling it. "Yes," she said. The love she felt for him hadn't died. It was like the flower that lies dormant for twenty years…then blooms. "That's where I belong, till—"

He nodded and their lips met again, and then they touched the tears on each other's faces and smiled.

"Let's get married," he said.

"Are you being impulsive?"

"Yes," he whispered.

"When?"

"As soon as we can get a license."

"I would like to ask my daughter."

His smile was wide in his beautiful face. "How do you think I knew what size ring to get you?"

Chapter 27

Nancy could hardly believe it. Her mom said, "It's about time. And I'm not talking about the clock." Yes, of course her mom would have known how she felt about Woody. She went to her mom and they hugged. Then her mom hugged Woody.

Jim said he expected it years ago, the way Nancy had chased poor Woody until he had to leave the country.

Rebekah topped them all. She said, "Mom never said I was too young to marry, so I won't tell her she's too old." She looked at Nancy then and said, "At your ages, you better go for it ASAP."

But they decided the same thing. They all attended the candlelight service at church. Nancy sat beside Woody. Their families took up the entire row. After the service, Woody and Nancy talked to Pastor Jameson.

Deciding to "go for it," they arranged to marry on Sunday after the worship service and invited the congregation and other friends to attend. They could have celebration receptions at the college or wherever they wanted later on.

Three days later, everything was in place for their wedding. The church was already decorated with greenery, a tree with lights, and colored ornaments. A manger scene graced one side, reminding them of the love of God, a love greater than humans could ever imagine.

Nancy had never been so aware of God's love and this blessing He was allowing her. To have had a life with a wonderful man. To begin a life with another.

Nancy carried a bridal bouquet of mini mauve calla lilies. She wore an ankle-length white gown and fingertip veil. She did not wonder what anyone might think of her wearing white. She was not tainted because she'd been married before. It had been a good marriage, sanctioned by God.

This was a new beginning, with Woody.

He wore a black tux with a calla lily boutonniere. He was looking at her the way she had hoped for so many years ago.

After the ceremony, they climbed into the backseat of Jim and Lauren's car. They would go to the Walkers' to change then have a family dinner at the Knight Hotel before going to Woody's condo for the night. Tomorrow they'd fly to Paris.

As Jim pulled away from the church an awful commotion sounded.

"What in the world?" Nancy said.

Lauren laughed. "Just a little getting back at you for what you did to the car when I married."

"Ach." Nancy and Woody both turned and looked out the back window. Huge bells attached to a chain, that someone must have tucked under the car, clanged and rang as they drove down the few blocks to her mom's house.

"Let us out in front of the house," Nancy said. She sent Woody a challenging look.

"You'll freeze," Lauren said.

"No way. I've got my love to keep me warm."

"And me." Woody climbed out.

"That's who I was talking about," she said.

"I sure hoped so," he said.

Although the dress was strapless and the veil didn't do much to cover her shoulders, Nancy did not feel cold. Woody knew exactly where she was taking him. Over to the maple tree.

"Where we first kissed," Woody said, and she saw the love in his eyes. There was no reserve now. This was like she was seventeen again and he was twenty-three. Only better.

"Love doesn't die," she said. "Sometimes it just has to wait."

"Christmas is a magical time," he said. "Miracles can happen. This is proof."

"Especially when a soft snow falls."

He looked up. "It *is* snowing."

His arms were already around her, and his lips nearing hers. She shrugged. "Let it snow."

* * * * *

REQUEST YOUR FREE BOOKS!

2 FREE CHRISTIAN NOVELS
PLUS 2
FREE
MYSTERY GIFTS

HEARTSONG
PRESENTS

YES! Please send me 2 Free Heartsong Presents novels and my 2 FREE mystery gifts (gifts are worth about $10). After receiving them, if I don't wish to receive any more books I can return the shipping statement marked "cancel." If I don't cancel, I will receive 4 brand-new novels every month and be billed just $4.24 per book. That's a savings of 20% off the cover price. It's quite a bargain! Shipping and handling is just 50¢ per book in the U.S.* I understand that accepting the 2 free books and gifts places me under no obligation to buy anything. I can always return a shipment and cancel at any time. Even if I never buy another book, the two free books and gifts are mine to keep forever.

159 HDN FVYK

Name _____ (PLEASE PRINT)

Address _____ Apt. #

City _____ State _____ Zip

Signature (if under 18, a parent or guardian must sign)

Mail to the **Harlequin® Reader Service:**
IN U.S.A.: P.O. Box 1867, Buffalo, NY 14240-1867

* Terms and prices subject to change without notice. Prices do not include applicable taxes. Sales tax applicable in N.Y. This offer is limited to one order per household. Not valid for current subscribers to Heartsong Presents books. All orders subject to credit approval. Credit or debit balances in a customer's account(s) may be offset by any other outstanding balance owed by or to the customer. Please allow 4 to 6 weeks for delivery. Offer available while quantities last. Offer valid only in the U.S.

Your Privacy—The Harlequin® Reader Service is committed to protecting your privacy. Our Privacy Policy is available online at www.ReaderService.com or upon request from the Harlequin Reader Service.
We make a portion of our mailing list available to reputable third parties that offer products we believe may interest you. If you prefer that we not exchange your name with third parties, or if you wish to clarify or modify your communication preferences, please visit us at www.ReaderService.com/consumerschoice or write to us at Harlequin Reader Service Preference Service, P.O. Box 9062, Buffalo, NY 14269. Include your complete name and address.

HSPDIR13

REQUEST YOUR FREE BOOKS!

2 FREE INSPIRATIONAL NOVELS
PLUS 2
FREE
MYSTERY GIFTS

Love Inspired

LIDIR13

ReaderService.com

Manage your account online!

- Review your order history
- Manage your payments
- Update your address

*We've designed
the Harlequin® Reader Service
website just for you.*

Enjoy all the features!

- Reader excerpts from any series
- Respond to mailings and
  special monthly offers
- Discover new series available to you
- Browse the Bonus Bucks catalog
- Share your feedback

Visit us at:

ReaderService.com

HEARTSONG

PRESENTS

Look out for 4 new
Heartsong Presents books next month!

**Every month 4 inspiring faith-filled
romances will be available in stores.**

These contemporary and historical Christian
romances emphasize God's role in every
relationship and reinforce the importance of
faith, hope and love.

To Trust or Not to Trust a Cowboy?

Former Dallas detective Jackson Stroud was set on moving
to a new town for his dream job, until he makes a pit stop
and discovers on the doorstep of a café an abandoned
newborn and Shelby Grace, a waitress looking for a fresh
start. He decides to help Shelby find the baby's mother,
and through their quest he believes he's finally found a
place to belong, while Shelby's convinced he will move on
eventually. What will it take to convince Shelby that this is
one cowboy she can count on?

Bundle of Joy
by
Annie Jones

Available March 2013!

Matchmaker—Matched!

For Ellie O'Brien, finding the perfect partner is easy—as long as
it's for the other people in the town of Peppin, Texas. When her
handsome childhood friend Lawson Williams jokingly proposes,
the town returns the favor and decides a romance is in order for
them. But when secrets in both their pasts threaten their future,
can the efforts of an entire town be enough to help them claim a
love as big and bold as Texas itself?

A TEXAS-MADE MATCH

by **Noelle Marchand**

Available in March wherever books are sold.